CHANGE OF HEART

Change of Heart

BY
HAROLD A. EHRENSPERGER

FRIENDSHIP PRESS
NEW YORK

Library of Congress Catalog Card Number: 54-6189

COPYRIGHT, 1954, BY FRIENDSHIP PRESS, INC.

Printed in the United States of America

For my father,
Charles Louis Ehrensperger,
and his cousin,
Anna Brochhausen —

with heartfelt thanks

CHANGE OF HEART

CHAPTER 1

$\mathbb{T}$HE WATER BUFFALOES were brought to the tap-tank at the corner of the park just as the gray light of dawn was being punctured by the first red glow of the morning. The daily washing of the beasts had to be gone through with, no matter what the day. On this day white-dhotied men seemed to be moving in even larger numbers than usual, their scarves and towels about their shoulders like flags of the Order of the Bath, indicating a ritual celebrated every morning about this time. Lines of shrouded sleeping bodies on the sidewalks and in each doorway began to come to life. The sleep of the night was over, and the movement of the day had started.

The sidewalk population of Calcutta was now in motion; the crowded-in dwellers in tenements called *chawls* had begun to stretch, scratch themselves, and clean their teeth by rubbing them with sticks. There was no talking, little sound except the hacking and spitting that inaugurates the day, as if the night had to be cleared from the throat where it had stuck in the rough misty coolness of the morning. Little sound could be heard except the distant temple bells ringing to awaken the gods and the occasional morning song of some worshiper on his way to do *puja* by offering milk or sweets to the gods. Even the pi-dogs, lean and bony,

1

scraggly mongrels that they were, had not yet mustered up energy to fight, as if waiting for clearer light to detect the decaying garbage or leaves dropped by the late night walker after he had eaten his *khana*.

Half-naked bodies were huddled together at the same tap with the buffaloes. As with one hand each splashed water again and again over his glistening body, the other hand embarrassingly pulled free the thin cotton loincloth that stuck to the hips. This produced a rhythmic movement, a kind of dance by the men at the small tank.

Calcutta was waking up to election day, not just any election day, but the first election day of a free country. The washing men at the tap would vote as free men, and the owners of buffaloes might even take advantage of the franchise to express the wish of all water buffaloes and their owners—more taps and more tanks for bathing and washing.

The night before, the men who carried the red flags had promised this, this and much more at a meeting on Dharamtala Street. The meeting had been held in the park that the British had named Wellington Square. The men had said that a vote for the Party would bring a place to live, more room, houses, buildings, roofs over their heads. A vote for the Party would mean food, enough to sustain the body, not just enough to keep it alive. A vote for change would mean a job for every man. The millions would be housed, clothed, fed, given jobs, and, most important of all, given something to live for, to beget and raise still more children—children who would be guaranteed a chance to live in the free world of a workers' paradise.

This was no distant dream. Elect the candidate of the

2

Party and the day after election would bring a new dawn. Miraculously taps would pour forth their water, houses would be provided to live in, and there would be work for every man. "The day of oppression, Comrades, is over," the speakers had shouted. "The day of the Western capitalist exploiter is past." The listeners had been told that the day of the imperialistic government extending the right hand to the Western Bloc and the left to the Eastern Bloc was gone. Day after tomorrow, the day after the election, would be the new day.

Congress as a governing body had failed, the Communists claimed again and again. After four years of feeble effort, the conditions under which more than three hundred million people lived had not been changed. Gandhi's India was the victim of exploitation by the native imperialists— the Tatas, the Carnegies of India, and the wealthy Birlas. "Arise, Comrades, throw off the yoke of oppression," the speakers in the park had said. "The day of deliverance is at hand, in your hand, in the ballot that you will put in the box at the polling booth. You can vote for your future, it is yours to choose. *Day after tomorrow will be different!*"

Like a Gatling gun the staccato sounds of the loud-speaker had filled the park. The blaring noise of lorries, some filled with Congress Party followers and others with the henchmen of independent parties, had not drowned out the blatant promises. They came like shots fired against the vulnerable body politic of the nation.

The Revolution was here! "Comrades, arise!" As simple as that! Put the ballot in the right box, Pandora's box, make a wish, and it would happen like magic. Magic like the marvelous effect of the compound of rubies, pearls, and

3

diamonds for brain troubles and rejuvenations advertised in the papers. The formula could be bought with a price. It was guaranteed to bring faith and hope to ten thousand million souls, worshipers of promises and believers in appeasement for both gods and men, whose food more often than not was grass.

On this momentous morning, the figure of an eighteen-year-old boy became rigid as he looked from the corner to the center of the park. He put his clean dhoti around him apron-fashion, guaranteeing in one gesture the natural modesty that all Indians feel. His wet loincloth slipped to the street. There before him were the park, the poles where the floodlights had been, the empty platform where the speaker had stood and on which afterward some fifty homeless bodies had slept to dream of the coming day. Day after tomorrow! Today, the day on which he was bathing, was the tomorrow—election day, the day of decision.

Nihar rubbed his thin legs harder, splashed more water on his lean body, and wrapped a scarf around his abundant black hair, which had fallen wet and greasy onto his face as he stooped to rub his feet. The park had become the place of promises, promises of reform by the Congress Party, of revolutionary change by the Communists.

Independence was to have brought Utopia. Yet the boy knew that Utopia had not come with independence. The speakers at school prize-distribution days and college convocations had all spoken of social responsibility, of the concern of the individual for his state, and of personal responsibility in a democracy. Democracy, the Welfare State—these had been the big words, the mighty words with which to fashion dreams. Yet they remained words, words in speeches, words without substance, words without meaning for the people. Nihar knew now that they were words that become real only with responsibility. Words bought at a cost, a cost that could be paid only in the coin of character! America had found that out. India was awakening to it.

Four years of independence had brought no miracles. Stones remained stones, they were not turned into bread. Men remained the pathetic and often miserable creatures they had been before, rich and poor, educated and uneducated. Most of them were selfish and unscrupulous, the inheritors of democracy that demanded an inheritance tax of character, which these victims of centuries of apathy and disillusionment could not pay. Calling on the gods or the stars did not bring them luck. There was no talisman or charm for this. The fault on this election day was still not in their stars but in themselves.

As the washers at the corner tap scrubbed and splashed, they little realized all of this. They had been told during these campaigning days about countries where the conditions of men had been changed, not because the men themselves had changed them, but because they had put their trust in a system that had worked. These systems were run by men the world called dictators. Food and clothes and houses and jobs could be bought with the price of freedom. Freedom, in a fashion, these men at the tap-tank had. This they could use to bargain with—it was their only coin. The more precious coin of character had not been minted in them, and so they could not barter with it. The Communists knew this.

Democracy could be bought only with character. Communism could be bought with personal and social freedom. Democracy asks personal and social responsibility. Communism asks submission, the herding of all wills into a common destiny that demands the willingness to be controlled rather than character to make personal decisions. All dictators know this. Dictators do not want character in a man, they know it is actually dangerous. What they want and must have, Nehru had warned, is the control of the will of man, the will that may be educated to choose, the will to differ, and, most of all, the will to aspire.

An easy bargain! What was this freedom anyway? For millions of men washing this morning in tanks and public taps in India, freedom was a nebulous something they could not feel nor know. They were told that under the British Raj they did not have it and that now they had it, independence had brought it. What was this freedom? Were there not now just as many exploiters? Their color might be different, and they might be dressed in dhotis or pajamas or Western pants rather than white drill shorts, but underneath were they not the same? The names, the big, important words like freedom, independence, and democracy, had not changed those in power!

Twenty-four hours from today! Today was election day, the day to choose, to sell freedom if they wanted to because it was all they had to bargain with. Today was election day, the day to vote for a new world. Just step right up, put a ballot in the right box and, hocus pocus, the new day would arrive—tomorrow, not five years from now, not when projected five-year plans of the Congress government would bear fruit because men had worked to make them succeed, but now. Vote for the system and get a new

6

leader. Submit, sit back, and wait, the change would come!
All this had been promised again and again.

Nihar had squashed his loincloth on the wet pavement
and with a series of beatings had satisfied himself that it was
clean for another day. He slung it over his shoulder as he
walked toward a tea stall in front of which was an iron
fence on which he hung the cloth. The pale, brown-sugared
tea was what he always had first in the early morning. It
was as regular as his bath and as invigorating in a different
way. The vagrant population of the city had suddenly collected around the stalls, beggars had taken up their regular
positions, and the day's pattern had formed.

The boy poured the tea into the saucer, blew on it, and
then sucked it down, repeating the process two or three
times until the small cup was drained. He tossed an anna on
the counter and went next door to the shop where the
panwalla had just made fresh *pan* packets, that piquant
combination of betel and spices enclosed in a folded leaf
that is universally enjoyed in India. The wet greenness of
the packets was inviting, and Nihar bought two, putting
them both into his mouth at once. The pleasurable taste
was recompense enough for the large mouthful that had to
be mastered, and it was only a few seconds before he was
able to spit a tremendous splash of red against the iron fence
post. As the bloodlike juice ran down the post and the cross-
pieces, it almost touched the drying end of his loincloth.
A tooth-cleaning on the way to the bath, the bath, the cup
of tea, and the *pan*—this was the regular routine that the
boy followed morning after morning.

Yet Nihar liked it. There was nothing restricted about
it. It was, in a very real way, the sense of freedom that he

7

enjoyed. He belonged to the spot where he had slept. He had paid for a space in a room with other men, but it was much too crowded and too hot to sleep there. He had been used to the open. He belonged to the tap where he washed and now to the park where he sat to enjoy the juicy chew. He had freedom. Freedom not to drink the tea at the same stall, to wash as long as he wanted to, to spit where he wished, freedom each morning for the half hour before he caught a bus to the jute mill where he worked for seven hours a day.

But today was different. He did not have to hang on to a bus. Today was election day, and the mill was closed. Today was his to vote for change. The men at the mill had told him it was their only hope.

Today in the park Nihar slid his dhoti around his body, put on the still damp loincloth, and then rearranged the dhoti carefully so that it held together outlining his slim hips. He remembered where he was to vote, and he wandered over to that side of the park only to be told that more than two hours remained before the polling place would open. Already the street was full of people. Everywhere there seemed to be policemen. An air of expectancy as if some tremendous change was about to take place buoyed him up. The police regulations had forbidden soliciting for votes within a few hundred feet of the polls, but workers of all parties were on hand. In this district only two candidates had been declared, the Congress candidate, who was the present Chief Minister of the State, and his Communist opponent, a vigorous and popular man, who was considered a serious threat as a vote getter.

Nihar sat on a bench near the open-air gymnasium where

8

on many nights he had watched boys of his own age boxing, doing bar bell exercises, or jumping ropes. He had often wished he might join them, but the fee for membership was fantastic in contrast with the little money he was getting at the mill. That was one of the things these speakers in the park had been talking about. In the U.S.S.R., said one man who had been there, free parks of "Rest and Culture" had been made available to all workers, and boys his age could play games as well as practice physical exercises.

One night soon after he had come to Calcutta two years before, Nihar had gone to a boxing match with Prabhu, a Hindu at the mill, and he had been tempted to go back again just to be with the boys and to feel some sense of belonging. This sports club was supported by a wealthy Hindu gentleman, and it was named after him. Prabhu was an enthusiastic member, and he had invited Nihar to go again. But Nihar was a Christian, and he had always meant to look around to see if the Christians had any such clubs. The drudgery of the mill and the routine of his life, however, had made him apathetic and lacking in initiative.

Shortly after the boxing match, another boy had invited him to a Communist meeting, and after that he had been absorbed night after night by the processions, the meetings, and the general excitement that made Calcutta continuously fascinating and made him forget the loneliness that had haunted him since he first came to the city. Never had Nihar experienced such excitement as he had seen in Calcutta just before this election. Today would end this excitement. He had dreaded to have this happen, for he knew of nothing that would take its place. The park this morning already had the atmosphere of the day after a picnic.

9

CHAPTER 2

Nihar had made up his mind how he would vote. His decision was not the result of considered reasoning based on the speeches he had heard. It was, rather, the result of tumultuous things that had happened to him without his maneuvering them. His decision had come full grown after an experience in this same park two weeks before.

It had been early evening, that feverish time of activity in India when the routine work of the day has been finished and the lingering light still gives time for buying—a bargaining process that is the chief recreation and the greatest skill of many of the people. Even more than at other times, early evening is the time of people. They seem to emerge from everywhere, some washed and groomed for the life that begins at this hour, some with bundles and packages, all active and more than ordinarily purposeful. People, people, people!

Wellington Square had been unusually crowded that night. The streets on the side with the tram cars had been cleared by the police so that the traffic of cars, carts, wagons, and lorries could pass. Police were everywhere, the regulars in their stiff khaki shirts and shorts, armed with long poles called *lathis* with which they kept back the crowd.

Within what seemed like only a few moments, thousands of men had suddenly formed into a crowd. From individuals and small groups, they were transformed into a mass.

10

Where there had been units of men in the park and in the street, there suddenly seemed to be one great, moving throng. Pressing forward toward a house, as if by the force of motion, like the force of a wave dashing against a rocky shore, this sea of white-dhotied and white-trousered men surged forward. These men were a curious lot. Their furtive glances backward, their self-conscious laughs, their incessant loud talking—these were all evidence of uncertainty, evidence that they had been caught in a movement and were suddenly being carried on with it, the individual unable to comprehend just what it all meant or where he was going.

A few had known. The cries and the slogans they shouted were taken up by the others until the whole mass was a yelling, pushing mob, yelling because those in front yelled, pushing because a house stood directly in front of them as an objective. A mob, formed so suddenly that no concerted, directed effort could have been responsible; a mob created spontaneously out of the masses of men in a crowded Indian city where individuals and groups breathe an air of expectancy polluted by disappointment and where forced leisure gives any incentive for attention a focus that soon develops men into a crowd.

This was not a mob of thousands of Communists, as the papers had reported, charging onto the home of the Chief Minister of the State who was the leader of the Congress Party. It was a mob of miscellaneous men suddenly galvanized into a mass made up of individuals who neither knew its reason for existence nor the attraction of B. C. Roy's house toward which it pressed. A mob made up of men who had time to be a mob because they had nothing

11

else to do or because they found that being a mob gave them incentive and purpose that they lacked as individuals. A mob that seemed suddenly to have mysterious direction, as each man who formed it lent his body and his voice to the push toward the common objective.

Five or ten men, joined through curiosity by others, jumped the iron fence around the park and started across the street toward the Minister's house. As if prearranged, passers-by as well as idlers in the park saw the little movement and came alive to something to do. In less than three or four minutes, men came running from all directions as if pulled toward some goal that had suddenly taken on magnetic powers.

Who had the individuals in this mob been? Men of India who had heard the promises of freedom without knowing the cost of freedom. Men piled on men in the cities, divorced from the soil where they belong, sleeping on sidewalks, washing at taps along the street, eating in the stalls set up in any vacant space. Men without roots except the grounding in the country where they had been born, expecting from it, now that it was free, a salvation that it never could fulfill. Men unwilling now through ignorance to guarantee that freedom through hard work, impotent before the overwhelming facts of India—disease, poverty, no chance for betterment. Disappointed men, slowly starving on the promises of leaders, alive because they had been fed by governments outside their own, sickening on the food because they knew it contained a poison of dependence from which they had revolted by jailing and sacrificing themselves. Men of India, lean and bony, looking at the well fed foreigner and contemptuous of him as the sign and symbol of the force that had held them down so long. Nihar had been a part of that excitement and that hatred.

The police and newspapers had called this a Communist riot. Communist? Perhaps the five or ten leaders who had watched the street and park were Communists. Instinctively or with a strategic sense, they had seized the moment of attack, the time of corralling. This had been prepared for by shouting slogans, the Communists shouting at the Congress followers who from time to time went into the house or stood about nervously on the pavement in front of it, obviously without anything to do but with an air of importance that deceived the idler into thinking each man was an official.

Nihar had learned the method of the Communists. Never a large number, they had become the strategists of the right moment. Their techniques were all geared to take advantage of the right moment so that a few could become the many. They were the leaders of the masses who lacked direction and purpose, masses waiting for the moment that would sweep them into action and carry them along. Their miserable condition and their wretched lives irritated them like an itching sore wanting to be scratched, a sore caused by a deeper infection that must first of all be cleaned out.

It had been fun, this yelling, this flaunting of one's defiance toward the citadel of established law and order. A crowd awed by some great catastrophe may stand still, or at least appear to, the constant movement of individuals within it being submerged into the larger group. But a mob is a movement, it can't stand still. The emotional force that impels it generates a restlessness within that gives it motion.

On that evening two weeks before Nihar had been a

body caught with a thousand other bodies in the park facing the house. He had not meant to be a part of a mob, he had just become one with it. Moved first by the action of the small group of men who had started toward the B. C. Roy house, he had found himself suddenly a part of them, a participant. In the excitement of the charge, he had found an exhilaration that lifted him and gave him purpose. His body suddenly bent to the push and flow of the crowd. His muscles became alive and his whole frame activated. His face took on life that made it full of expression and gave it a beauty that had almost been erased in the meaningless quality it had assumed at the mill. This was fun! This was something to do!

Back of Nihar a group of boys his own age had rushed into a pole that had been erected in the park for floodlights and for the loud-speaker during political meetings. The heaving mass of bodies pressed against the pole until it swayed. It, too, might move and move with force. He turned and pushed himself toward the pole. A boy leaped toward it and, grabbing it, swung himself around it, screaming his delight in the zestful motion. The boy's knees and feet hit Nihar in the stomach, and he grabbed the bare legs and held them up as the boy pulled himself higher and higher.

The pole swayed still more, and a wire attached to the top of it snapped. It might be a live wire! When this idea was born in the minds of the men, they began a mad scramble to get away from it. But the boy held on and climbed still higher. In the excitement of this frenzied Maypole dance, the crowd again forced the pole and it toppled, the body of the boy on it falling with it into the arms of Nihar.

14

A wild shout went up from the crowd. A pole, a pole, what one could not do with it! Nihar, the boy, and fifty others seized it and started forward, phalanxlike. The loudspeaker of the police officers' car was shouting in Bengali that the street must be cleared or the police would charge the crowd. In five minutes! The men were too excited to listen. Some in front had started back toward the park, frightened by the angry gestures of the police as they swung their sticks. This only intensified the melee, and the sport of pushing and pulling became all the more enjoyable.

A loud explosion, followed immediately by a second shot, brought everyone to attention. Someone must have thrown a bomb! The mob took on the violence of the outburst and within a second seemed to be an unmanageable mass. The police captain gave the order to charge! A hundred police from lorries, from the sides of other houses, suddenly appeared with *lathis* and began charging into the crowd. The roar was tremendous. A wave of humanity started to move across the park, the younger men and boys jumping over benches and path markers, stumbling and falling, pushing and shoving. The Calcutta police had maneuvered such a clearance before. With amazing speed they again had forced back what seemed to be thousands of men. The retreat became a stampede!

The little park was surrounded by a high iron fence, the fence on which Nihar had often hung his dhoti. On the four sides were gates, once equipped with turnstiles, giving the only openings onto the streets. Years before, at a certain decorous time of the night the gates had been closed and the park cleared. But with the passing of the British Raj, Wellington Square had become the center for political

15

meetings, and the turnstile had long since disappeared. The strong iron fence and the narrow exits to the street still remained. The mob had pushed against a fence, forcing itself through a narrow gate, looking for all the world like white sticky frosting with dirty specks in it oozing out of a pastry tube.

The more athletic men on that day two weeks before had jumped the fence, no little feat when one wears a dhoti. But dhotis can be pulled up around the hips, leaving the feet and legs free. Over the cries and shouts of the mob, the sound of crashing sticks had been heard. Occasionally in the fights that ensued there had been a more ominous sound, the thud that made one know a head had been hit.

With the rest of the men and boys, Nihar had dropped the pole, which now lay on the ground to trip hundreds of feet in the rush. Shins had been cracked, toes stubbed, arms and bare bodies scratched and bruised. Miraculously, Nihar had reached the opposite side of the park. At his side, clinging to his dhoti, was the boy who had climbed the pole and whose body had landed in his arms. In his excitement Nihar scarcely noticed him except to be aware that he was a youngster. When they reached the high iron fence with its pointed, spiked top, the boy leaped up the fence rails as swiftly as if he were climbing a coconut palm. On top he balanced precariously, his slim body naked except for a loincloth. As he stopped to take hold of the iron paling, he reached his other hand to Nihar and pulled him up. Without knowing quite how either of them did it, they found themselves jumping together from the top of the fence.

When they landed, their feet stinging from the jump,

16

they ran silently down the middle of the street past Lee Memorial, a refuge for orphans near the far end of the square. Here they stopped at the little tank and tap that Nihar had used so many mornings.

In less than five minutes the park became empty, with dull yellow lights casting a strange glow over the place. As Nihar had looked back, he could see here and there the evidences of the battle—a piece of white dhoti caught on a post, a paper torn to shreds in the scramble of feet, the overturned *chula* of the peanut seller with the hot coals still smoking on the ground, and, in two or three places, clusters of soldiers and police bending over a figure that had been clubbed too hard. But the street opposite was completely bare, the park was empty, and an ominous and frightening silence settled down over street and park, the quietness of an approaching storm, the dead stillness of delayed anticipation.

Down the narrow alleys and the wider streets a thousand Bengalis had fled, dispersed like an army of rats. The police examined their own arms and legs, took account of their sticks, and moved together to form a line for inspection by their captain. They had been proud of their accomplishment. And from the balconies of houses looking onto the square, eager faces had watched the performance, remembering in their moment of excitement other charges in this park, other bombs exploded, shots that had come too close to their houses and had made all living a jittery, moment-by-moment existence.

The boy who had attached himself to Nihar that day was one of the multitude in India who come from what is now called the Scheduled Classes. Gandhi affectionately

17

called them the Harijans, the ones God loves. With their hands, Nihar knew well, the dirty work of the nation was done. They were not an insignificant number, but they were still unable to rise above the miserable condition they had known all their lives, a condition into which they had been born and from which they would go when they died. In the short or long expanse of life, no change seemed possible. This had been their destiny until the new Constitution proclaimed a casteless society. In time they could now hope to be free of their age-long stigma.

At the corner of the square, the boy had released his hold on Nihar's hand and disappeared in the crowd, lost in the enveloping figures of the city, part of its rush, its noise, its impersonal unrelatedness.

As Nihar had walked that night to the Maidan, the great central park of Calcutta, he wished the boy might have stayed with him. He longed to talk with someone, he wanted to know and be known by someone. As it was he knew no one, and no one knew him. He was part of the anonymous mass of a great city.

But he liked the city just because it was so different. He had been told that Calcutta was almost the only city where there had been election riots preceding the first election when 176,000,000 people would vote for the first time. How glad he was to be in this unpredictable city, in the territory of the Bengalis, who were always explosive and exciting.

When he had reached the busiest corner of the metropolis, Nihar had stood watching its motley population. Most of them were unaware of the fact that a half mile away there had been a riot. By this time he had become composed again, and the people and the noises distracted him so that the excitement of the street was substituted for the nervous revolution of the park. As he had waited, his eyes caught sight of the papers and magazines spread out on the pavement to his left. He wandered over to them and soon became absorbed by their gay covers and graphic pictures and exciting headlines of stories of the new world born of Communism. For a few annas he could buy a wonderful collection of reading matter. Almost automatically he had taken from his dhoti the annas and purchased a book and a magazine. He went to sit in the park near a lamp and read. More important, that night he decided he would vote for the transforming system.

CHAPTER 3

COMMUNISM APPEALED to Nihar for somewhat the same reason that Christianity had appealed to the people in his village in Bihar. With them he belonged to one of the lower castes in the Indian social system. He had accepted this as a recognized fact, a fact from which there was no escape. Yet the villagers had been rescued, or so they thought, because they had become the followers of the One who declared that God loves all men and that all are equal in his sight. Communism, Nihar decided, offered a political system that might implement their ideas about God. As he sat in Wellington Square election morning, he thought about his village.

19

His father owned a small tract of land, and Nihar had grown up on it, helping in one way or another for as long as he could remember. He recalled a feeling of belonging with the oxen his father owned. He had learned to harness them with the knotted rope that had done duty long after it might have been thought worthless. He had watched his father beat the animals with a stick, knowing that his brother and his father had been kinder to their dumb beasts than most of the neighbors had been. He remembered one day when he himself was driving the oxen back home from the threshing place in the center of the village. They were more stubborn than usual, having gone round and round the floor tramping out the grain until they seemed to know no other direction, and they insisted upon walking off the road. Only that one time had he done what he had seen other men do often, twist their tails, twist them until the lumbering animals gave a start, the reaction to the sharp pain they felt.

What he could never forget were the endless days he had sat on the *machan*, that crude, elevated platform of bamboo and straw, watching the ripening grain, shooing away the thieving birds who came to feast. He was first taken there by his elder sister, perched on her hip with his legs clinging viselike to her body so that his hips and thighs became strong long before the muscles of his legs strengthened into braces to hold up his growing body. He could also remember the exciting times when he had taken his father's *khana*, usually some cold flat bread and vegetables, to the fields. While his father ate and rested, he guided the rude wooden plow behind the oxen, feeling himself pulled by its irregular jumpy motion. He remembered, too, the happiness

20

he had known on his way back to the village when he stopped in the jungle to eat fruits, an intuition telling him which ones were good and which were not. He recalled the first pice—only one-fourth of an anna—he had earned, selling some peanuts he had found on the ground after the men had pulled the stocks and taken them away. Tucking the peanuts in his dhoti, he had bargained with the merchant who finally bought them. These were the first fruits of his labor, a kind of work that his family had known so long. It must have been soon after this that he decided his own efforts would be more efficient and productive if they were different.

The stirring of this desire to change his life had come early to Nihar. He could scarcely remember when it had begun. But he did recall vividly the day the strange sahib appeared. For that was the name they gave the man, even though he was not British. He came to the village seeking men who were willing to go to Calcutta to work in the jute mill. Nihar himself was too young to go then, but as he listened to this man, he felt sure that sooner or later he would go to the big city. A good wage was promised—more than two rupees a day—and a place to live in the company houses, a clinic where medical care could be had, and a chance to live in the city.

Calcutta! What a thrilling experience! Movies, melas—fairs—bigger than any he had ever known, bazaars packed with everything anyone could imagine, and freedom—freedom to do as he wanted, to wander where he chose, to live! In the city he hoped he might be able to save enough money to continue his schooling. Yes, that was what the sahib had suggested. And there were also men there, in

21

Calcutta, who could help him—padre-sahibs, learned men who ran schools. Nihar had become determined to go to Calcutta.

Long before this he had looked forward to the melas that were held each year by both Hindus and Christians. These days were the biggest of the year for him, days he waited for. Months were spent in preparation for them. The humdrum life of the village consisted of daily chores, which began at five in the morning with the feeding of the oxen, goats, and sheep. Often he had to be called from a happy interlude of the game called *gill danda*, played with stones and sticks, to take the cattle to the grazing field, which during the dry season was a long distance from the house.

Then the time for the mela would come, and for him the mela became what he thought Calcutta would be like every day. There he would see higher stacks of clay pots and pans called *dechies*—more than he had ever seen in his life. There would be more of the gleaming brass, which always attracted the village women and to which he also found himself drawn. There would be cloth, even in the times of scarcity, beautiful cloth that the men said came from far-off Lucknow or the mills of Nagpur, cloth that might mean a new sari he could buy for his mother and sister and a new dhoti for himself. Nihar remembered how his mother always saved her best sari for the mela, but it had been worn so long and had been pounded and pommeled so much in the washing that it was discolored and torn. In Calcutta he might get her a new sari for the mela and Nihar would be glad, glad just to have freshness in the cloth, bright colors, and the mysterious figures printed on the cloth, which

22

told the name of the mill and the price of the cloth per yard. Nihar often wished, too, that he might have a new dhoti rather than shorts made of the cut-off pieces from one of his father's discarded ones. He wanted a white dhoti with the figures still left on, a design of fashion, store bought and flaunting newness.

Yet for Nihar the village mela had also meant something much more important. He loved the songs, the *bajans*. The white sahib who had come into the village had taught them to sing. The boys danced, too, falling into steps and rhythm that had come down in the village for longer than the oldest man could remember.

There were mysterious evenings when the singing continued the whole night. The Christians were not to be outdone by their Hindu neighbors who had *puja* celebrations for even longer periods. Many people came, people he had never seen before, new people and new faces, boys whose strangeness lent attractiveness, whose bodies were to be tested and compared in skills and games. Distant villages sent teams, competitors who aroused in him a spirit he did not know was there and, when he won, a sense of importance that made him sure that some day he would do the things he dreamed of.

Some of the things he had wanted to do he had not dared to admit. Secretly, as he sat watching the animals grazing or as he doodled in the crowded class of the village school, he dreamed of taking part in the play that had been introduced into the mela by the missionary sahib.

Year after year as these melas had come and gone, his father said sternly that they had no religious value. True, there were speeches, long ones that never seemed to end, punctuated in his own case by his need to move about, excuses he devised for leaving the meeting, and the fun of being joined by other boys who loitered as they returned to the crowd of people facing the preacher. The missionary sahib said that the village melas were too "secular"—a word Nihar never understood—that they had formerly been occasions of great religious revival. Nihar had heard stories of the conversions—his own grandfather's had been one—of the baptisms in the river, and of the renewed religious interest in the village when the mela was over.

That must have been a long time ago. In more recent melas there had been only things to buy, fun in the games, and boys whom he would not see again until the next year. Then one year something new happened. About three months before the time of the mela, the missionary sahib came riding into the village in his jeep. With him was another man. The padre-sahib of the village rushed out to greet them and after him the boys and men who had not gone out into the fields. Nihar did not understand all that was said, but he knew it was important because it had an important sound. He caught the word "mela" and what he thought was "play."

At last after tea, the visitors met the village men under the big banyan tree in the padre's yard. The boys sat at the edge of the group to catch the words that flew off the whirl of conversation. There was to be a play, like the plays he had seen the Hindus do at Diwali, a play, the visitors had said, about Jesus Christ!

Nihar could remember the moment he had first heard this announcement. It strangely warmed him, sending a sudden thrill up and down his spine. Like all Indian boys and girls,

24

he had play-acted. He could not remember when he hadn't! He enjoyed it more than games, he believed, more than talking to the boys at the mela, more even than flying kites and winning by cutting down the best kite in the neighborhood. The men talked about the play, about the disciples, about the last days of Jesus' life, about the plans for the practice, about the fact, the glorious fact, that the white sahib would come back a week later to manage the play, direct it Nihar had thought he heard them say.

"We will want the best men and women of the village to play in it," the visitor said. "Characters will be chosen by the padre and the committee. In the West where I come from, there is a famous village where a great play about the life of Christ is put on. The characters in this play are chosen by the villagers themselves, chosen because in their daily lives they have shown that they are worthy of playing the great roles that these lives represent. We must have a Peter, a Mary Magdalene, Mary, the mother of Jesus, and Jesus. Think what it will mean for one of you to act Jesus!"

Nihar's eyes had never revealed a greater depth. They were wide in excitement, pools of darkness in which lay a yearning that was suddenly stirred.

"But the character next to Jesus, the man who was closer to the heart of Christ than anyone else was John, John the Beloved Disciple," the white sahib went on.

Nihar's heart leaped up. He could remember how as his father had learned to read he had been particularly eager to know about these disciples who were close to the great Prophet and especially about this one disciple closer than all the rest.

John, the Beloved Disciple! Nihar suddenly stood up.

25

He looked at his body, on down to his long legs. He was sixteen then, tall for his age, strong and firm. He looked from his body to the white man who had been talking. John, the Beloved Disciple, the man closest to Jesus—that was the part he wanted to play! He did not dare then say this out loud, but, as he looked at his legs and feet, he was saying with his whole self that he wanted to be the Beloved Disciple, that he wanted his body suddenly to become John, that he would grow up quickly and effectively to be worthy of the part.

Nihar watched the play that year with particular interest. It brought new life into the mela. It was, in fact, the center of interest in the entire mela. Nihar was not chosen to play a part, not even a boy in the Jewish crowd, but he found that he could be useful in the preparation of the play. His father because he was a carpenter made the cross, a crude one, to be sure, since that was what they wanted. Nihar took the cross from the shop where for days men and boys had watched his father working on it, to the place where nightly the missionary rehearsed the play. Nihar helped in other ways, too, because the sahib said that everyone in the village not in the cast could have a part in the play, the girls and the women in arranging the costumes, the men and boys in helping with the staging.

What fun it had been to carry the cross to the rehearsal space! Nihar watched his good friend Prem, a young man of twenty-one, who had been selected to play the part of Simon the Cyrenian, the man who carried the cross of Jesus. As Prem took the cross back and forth to the stage, dragging its heavy weight behind him, Nihar made up his mind that even though he himself might never lead a life

26

good enough to be worthy of playing John, the Beloved Disciple, he could someday at least be Simon and carry the cross.

The play that year had meanings for Nihar that he felt were all his own. He had always heard about these men and women in the Bible story, but now they suddenly became alive, suddenly were as real as the person seated on the ground next to him. It was not just the change of their dhotis and their saris into clothes that he had always seen in Bible pictures. It was not the dazzling light of the glaring Petromax lamps that had been set at the sides where some of the boys pumped them to keep the kerosene burning brightly. It was not even the scant scenery that transported him from the rude countryside of India to the country outside of Jerusalem. It was something else, some magic that made him feel an excitement and a joy that he had never felt before. A man from the neighboring village was the Christus, his own father the high priest, and the young man who had given Nihar his first top John, the Beloved Disciple. Nihar had always had a sense of close relationship to this man long after his father had copied the top and made many tops like it for the other boys to spin.

Magic it must have been because Nihar could never quite explain it. All he knew then was that as he sat watching the play he was lost in another age and in a distant and strange country. At the same time he was also walking with these strangers, walking with them in those frightening and precarious days when closeness to the Galilean meant danger and possible death. He wished that the play might never end, even though it lasted long into the early morning hours. It was not long enough. He wanted it to go on.

Some day he would be John! He could come back after he had worked in Calcutta, and then he would be John. He would walk into this play in the presence of all the men and women with whom he had grown up, and they would walk with him and talk with him in the play and through the play and out of the play again into the village, and John would be alive, alive for all the people for as long as any would remember. These people might not learn to read, nevertheless the pages of Scriptures would suddenly be real to them. They could look and listen, year after year, so that the spirit of Jesus would become a living thing to them and the characters in the story would come alive. He would come back, he would be John. That Nihar had known as he had known few things in the confusing and changing life that he had lived as a young Indian in a village in Bihar.

Nihar came to himself with a start. Bihar in 1947! Four years ago. How he had changed! Now on this election morning while he had been sitting waiting for a chance to vote, how strange it was that he should have remembered his home, his family, and his desire to play the part of John. He shook himself suddenly, stretching in the bright sunlight, which had now initiated a hot and windless day. His dhoti almost fell to the ground as he arose. He pulled it close around him and twisted it tightly at the waist. Across the street in Lee Memorial, the men were lining up to vote.

As if he would run from this past that he had resurrected, Nihar started quickly toward the voting place. The men who were there were mostly young, a few about his own age and the rest in their middle or late twenties. They joked and talked as they pushed forward, their faces eager to see the gate into the big building open. Nihar felt a new importance, a sense of having grown up quickly like his young country, which was now adult and exercising its first franchise.

Two weeks before, just after the riot, he had made up his mind how he would vote. The party that had been in power had effected none of the changes he had hoped for. It was a symbol of failure with its unemployed loafers, with the continuous stream of people who were eking out an existence that was scarcely above the level of an animal. He would vote for a change!

The iron gates of the building where the voting would take place were now being opened by the police. The voters pushed until they felt their bodies one against the other, a solid line pressing toward the place where they would cast the ballot by putting it into the box. Nihar enjoyed this human line, it warmed him and gave him a sense of relationship with the rest of the men. Closer now and closer, he moved up the steps, into the school hall, out into the expanded, metal-enclosed porch so characteristic of all white sahib's places, up to the table where the ballot was. He was checked off. His registration was valid. All he needed to do now was vote.

He looked down the boxes on which the symbols of the parties had been pasted until his eye saw the sickle and the sheaf. He hesitated, intrigued by the other symbols. Then he took his ballot and held it over the box. It was suddenly out of his hands, he had voted. He heard the ballot scratch against the other ballots as he let it fall. He had voted! He had voted for a change! He had voted Communist!

The long period of two years in Calcutta had never seemed more important to Nihar than at that moment. Why had he thought about his home on this particular morning? Why had he thought about the Christian mela and, particularly, about the play? What a stupid, silly idea it had really been to think of playing John, the Beloved Disciple. He had given his allegiance to something more than the dim ideal he had remembered in the Galilean figure. He had grown up, and with his feeling of adulthood, he had made choices, choices that were his own. He had a new god in the Party— and he had become its beloved disciple!

CHAPTER 4

ONE DAY SOON AFTER the election Nihar was assigned to check the jute bundles that were brought from the river boatmen to be inspected and graded by the more expert workers at the batching floor. Most of the people with whom he worked seemed dull and listless, uninviting even if they had offered to be friendly with him. As he stood checking the long jute stalks, he became aware suddenly of someone near him who was looking at him. It was a girl. She stood nearby without saying anything, started to move away, then turned and smiled at him. That was all that happened, but in India and for Nihar that was a lot.

Another day at the "siesta" time—a period between ten-thirty in the morning and two in the afternoon—Nihar met a Hindu boy named Vinod who spoke to him, asking where he came from, how long he had been in the mill, and the other questions that always serve to introduce strangers, give them something to talk about, and make meeting a new acquaintance such a delightful experience.

One morning about a week later, wandering aimlessly out to the river in the mill compound, he met Vinod. He had noticed that this boy seemed to know many of the other workers and that he had some sort of office in the company union. This would be a chance to talk with him. It was obvious, though, that Vinod was not looking for him, and even before Nihar could get into conversation with him, he saw the girl who had smiled at him.

Vinod greeted her with enthusiasm.

"Hello," he called as he came to her. Then he turned toward Nihar, and with a gesture that took Nihar by surprise, he said, "This is Nihar. He comes from a village in Bihar. This is Nanda, Nihar, Nanda the wise one."

Nanda was self-conscious. She really felt as if she already knew Nihar.

"From Bihar? Where's that?" Her question was silly, she knew, but she had nothing to say.

"Bihar? The land of the famine—that's Bihar!" Vinod blurted out.

Nihar wanted to protest, but he seemed to find no words.

"He's Christian," said Vinod without waiting for Nanda to show any curiosity. "He fell for the company's line about coming to Calcutta to work. He has been in the city a little over two years."

"Nice of you, uncle, to take such an interest!" said Nanda.

"Another prospect?" She looked at Nihar and then at Vinod.

"I've invited him to the club, if that is what you mean. He can meet some of the fellows there."

"And incidentally, just by chance, learn a thing or two?" Nanda laughed at this and walked away from the two boys down toward the river. Nihar had never been the center of attention like this. What was happening? This seemed like a dissection, a taking apart of himself without his being able to do anything about it. He wanted to say something, but he was sure that if he spoke his words would sound foolish. He wanted most of all to tell Vinod and Nanda how glad he was to be with them. He didn't care whether Vinod took him to a club or not. He was happy to be here now talking with someone.

Nihar wondered about this girl who looked different from anyone he had ever seen before. Where did she come from? The many confusing faces and the variety of types of people he had seen in Calcutta were unlike anything he had known. She was still more puzzling. He must ask about her. Now that she had walked away, he could talk to Vinod about her.

"Where's she from?" he began.

"A daughter of Lanka, a daughter of the Buddha—Ceylonese! Her father was probably Indian, and her mother Burmese for all I know. She never says much about her."

Nihar's wonder was even greater. He had never met anyone from Ceylon. It seemed as far away as Africa or Java. He had never met a Buddhist! He shrank within himself. People were always something else, Hindus or Muslims, and now this girl was a Buddhist. Were there no Christians in Calcutta?

Vinod left Nihar to go to the water's edge where Nanda

was sitting. They began an earnest conversation during which both of them looked at the magazine that Nanda had taken from her pocketbook.

Nihar was happy even if he had been left alone. He had met two people, they had recognized him, and he had talked with them. His loneliness seemed to leave him. For one ecstatic moment he had been with people as he had not been with them in the huge crowds in the city. He was happy. That afternoon time passed quickly. When he left the mill at four-thirty, he hoped that Nanda or Vinod would be waiting for him.

He lingered at the mill gate until he saw Vinod coming. He was about to walk up to him when Nanda appeared. The two walked off together, and the *namaste* he was about to utter never really came out. It remained unsaid like so many greetings he had wanted to give to boys and girls he had seen. These greetings remained unexpressed. They showed only in the appealing eagerness of his dark eyes, which more than once become moist with tears without his realizing it. This expression of anticipation was followed by the frustration that is the genesis of loneliness.

Loneliness! The gnawing appetite he felt for things that had never seemed important to him before in his village. The need for someone to talk with, to do the little inconsequential things for, to touch. He had touched people in the crowds. Yes, that must have been the reason he enjoyed standing in a crowd, pushing against the man in front of him until they were both conscious of each other. This was the touch born out of loneliness, eager tendrils of affection which he had never known he possessed but which now reached out and found no proper support for their tender grasp. The boys he had seen walking together hand in hand, as Indians like to do, recalled to him his friends at home. The two or sometimes three men riding side by side on cycles with their arms around each other became for him an attraction he might enjoy if only he could know someone in this overwhelming mass of people.

He must get to know Vinod better. Yes, that was what he wanted. Vinod was a young man who knew things, who talked freely with girls, who belonged to something that seemed to bring purpose and meaning into his life. He wanted Vinod as his friend.

As he watched his newly anticipated companion walking away with this strange Ceylonese girl, Nihar wanted to stop them. But he was confused as to which of them he wanted most as a friend. He was afraid of Nanda. Vinod would be safer. He would choose Vinod. And with this idea playing about in his mind, Nihar set out to follow them until they took a bus and disappeared in the direction of the city. Nihar decided suddenly that he must have tea. There was a new importance in his life. He had made an acquaintance. He would celebrate by having tea.

That night he walked the streets, sat in a park, and stood on street corners as if he were looking for someone, as if he expected someone. People, he felt sure, would think he was waiting for a friend. This was the beginning of the game he played with his unseen companion, the comforting escape from the pain and longing of loneliness, from his starvation for affection. He was waiting for a friend.

Playing at waiting for a friend was play-acting in the face of the grim reality of loneliness, the stark and terrible loneliness that a boy can feel in a big city, loneliness in the midst of thousands of people. Because of it Nihar stopped that night to look at a family of Kalimpong people who had set up housekeeping at the edge of the Maidan. They had built a fire over which they had placed pots in which boiled steaming rice. The old man of the family sat smoking what must have been a broken *hookah*, the long stem of the pipe no longer gracefully curved. The coarse clothes of the people seemed to weigh down their already solid, heavy bodies. In this most public of all places they were going about their business even to feeding the baby with little concern for the hundreds of passers-by who stopped to look, crowding in so close that blankets were stepped on. No one even questioned his right to see. The life of these strangers was everybody's business, and why not? The spectator became one with the crowd, laughing with it in the amusing intimacy that the crowd enjoyed, and the family did not seem to mind.

Waiting for someone whom he didn't know led Nihar to stop another night to listen to a half-naked sadhu with a dhoti around his middle on which were printed verses from the Bhagavad-Gita. Another night he stood for more than an hour watching a medicine man who had a mixture for the eyes. With a sweeping gesture the medicine man grabbed a boy, held him to him, and then with the movement of a dancer swished some of the liquid into his eyes while the boy stood prominently and conspicuously important before the wondering crowd. Back of the stand on which there were many bottles of the mixture stood a young, pale-faced boy singing in a falsetto voice what must have been the virtues of the medicine. The "doctor" himself uttered no words. Suddenly he would withdraw

35

from the boy he had treated and stand with his hands poised in the air as if he had stopped in the midst of directing an orchestra. Then again he would step forward and, with a grand gesture, grab another victim who might at first draw back or protest but who most of the time yielded to the healing power of the man through the magic mixture.

Nihar had thought that night about the doctor with the clean, white clothes who had come to his village. He remembered how the people had flocked to see him and how he examined each one of them and talked to them. Then with a healing benediction even in his voice, the doctor sent them away with Western medicine and a new confidence that the trouble could be overcome if only they would keep clean, watch the mosquitoes, and try to do something about the ever-present flies. As a boy Nihar had looked longingly at the village doctor, wondering if one day he himself might not come back to his village to help and heal. Now he seemed strangely to be a long way from that intention, yet as he watched the faces of the people around him, he saw yearning for help and need for healing in the ugly looking skin eruptions, in the watery eyes, in the emaciated bodies that were exposed before him. In those moments he forgot his own loneliness in concern about the needs of others.

Looking was free, and Nihar knew it. He spent hours just looking, storing up images for recollection when darkness made seeing impossible. Looking, he found, was tiring, too. After he made the long trek back to the workers' lines at the mill, he was worn out. To prepare for bed he needed only to take off his shirt, wrap his other old dhoti around his body, and lie down on the mat he had always carefully rolled up and put high up in the rafters toward the ceiling.

It was safer there from the rats and vermin that infested the place. He went to sleep quickly so that the snoring men did not disturb him.

He did not even wake up when the man sleeping next to him came in drunk on the night of the weekly payday. At first Nihar had often wakened to hear the men, cursing as they fell over the other bodies, belching and fuming from the food and drink they had consumed. Sleep was a saving grace. He could fall asleep again easily, and he had to be awakened in the morning by the men to get his face washed at the tap where they all crowded around and splashed, their unresponsive bodies deadened by the dirt floor on which they slept and the encrusted dust that never seemed to get quite washed off. It filled the cracks in the skin, enlarging them so that the legs of the older men looked like the rough skin of a cow or the still more coarse hide of the water buffaloes.

This crowded *chawl* bred intimacy, nothing was private. Yet it also seemed to inoculate the men against affection and concern. Each man's mat or burlap sack was his kingdom. No hand went from one to the other to help. The sick man was shunned because what he had might be contagious. Until he could muster enough strength to get to the clinic at the mill, he usually lay abandoned. At first Nihar had tried to help, but he soon found the time between getting up and signing in at the mill so short that he could not stop. He fell unconsciously into the pattern of unconcern. The more he wandered the streets at night looking for a friend, the more he resolved not to go back again to the *chawl*.

Soon Nihar began to sleep now and then in a doorway or in a park, returning to the *chawl* only to check on his small box filled with his unimportant collection of personal belongings. One night he loitered at a carnival where he enjoyed the exhibitions on the outside of the tents. He had a hidden desire to join the carnival, to become a part of its family of freaks and fakes, its animals, and its human derelicts. The inertia that kept him wandering also kept him from making a move to do any of the things he dreamed about.

He had been bewitched by a magician that night, and as he watched him, he was intrigued by the man's attraction for him. The dirty cards he flipped were fascinating, the black scarf used to cover an empty glass that suddenly became full of water and the small wand that needed to be waved over each and every trick seemed to him to be part of a world he did not know, a world of the strange, the unnatural, and the mysterious. He had even been pressed into service as one of the stooges used by the magician. Nihar had felt silly as he held the turban of the "doctor" and found it suddenly filled with flimsy silk squares that were pulled out one after the other to the gaping amazement of the crowd.

He knew that he must be blushing all over. Just as the trick ended, he looked out at the crowd and saw the laughing faces of Nanda and Vinod. His confusion at being recognized made him want to disappear as mysteriously as had a rabbit the magician whisked away. Yet at the same time he felt an overwhelming sense of happiness that the friends he had been waiting for had come. Unexpected, to be sure! But they had come!

Nanda called to him first. Her hands held books, she always seemed to be holding books. Then Vinod took his hand. It was the first time anyone had taken his hand since he had said good-by to his close friend Mohanlal when he left his village. A tenderness that he had almost forgotten was awakened in him, and he was happy.

"A new job?" Vinod was enjoying Nihar's confusion.

"Come along with us. We're going to a meeting. We can give you something better than tricks." Nanda's voice was pleasant and appealing.

"Tricks are what they want," Vinod said grandiosely. "Tricks, magic! Astrology and palmistry. It's the bunk!"

"Would you believe it? My father had my horoscope read," continued Nanda. "He wanted to have it ready against the fateful day when he might make the right match for me. I still have it."

"*Acha!* Suppose I have mine made? The trouble is that I don't know the time of the day when I was born, and that's important." Vinod enjoyed this bravado.

He had pushed both of his companions out of the crowd, and Nihar found himself walking with them. He had never heard people talk like this. It was exciting.

"We don't believe in that sort of thing," Nihar ventured to say as they walked.

"What do you mean, 'we'?" asked Vinod with a sarcastic tone in his voice. Nihar was silent. Somehow it seemed strange to say "We Christians" even though he knew that both of his friends accepted him as Christian.

"There is only one 'we,'" Vinod went on, "and that is all of us. We, the people, the masses, all the people around us. These labels and all the rest don't matter. The struggling masses of the world do. Belong to them, and you belong to the future."

Nihar was confused as they walked down Dharamtala Street with people dodging back and forth across the sidewalk, some pushing over into the street. He saw the tall building of the Salvation Army and still farther down a church. Both of these might have been a refuge for him, both belonged to what he knew was his background. Yet he had never been in either one. He had crossed the street one night when he saw the Salvation Army singers on a corner. Now he seemed to be catapulted into something else. He was going to a meeting, not because he had chosen to go, but because a will had come against his, a will alive to something that he did not know. By its very strength he was being pushed toward the unknown. Perhaps he ought to fake an excuse to enter the Salvation Army hall or say that he had an engagement. Perhaps he was too willing. He wondered whether Vinod and Nanda would think he was too eager. He didn't know. All he did know was that he had found friends for whom he had been waiting and that their presence on either side of him gave him an incentive to hurry on. He felt happy to be with people who talked to him. At last he belonged!

The crowded hall where the meeting was held was stifling. Nihar pushed his way in and found himself again a part of a crowd. Even if he could not understand, the intensity of what was being said seemed to spread from body to body. The fringe of men standing around those seated in the middle of the room on the floor seemed to be buoyed by a kind of energy that was being pumped into them by the speaker. Nihar had seen crowds before come completely under the power of a sadhu as he sang. He had watched them sway to the rhythm of the voice and join unself-consciously in the experience of the happy moment of fellowship—fellowship not so much with one another as with the very spirit of the song.

This was something very different. The louder the man spoke, the more intense the crowd became. Something seemed to be developing. Even though they had come in late, he found that they became a part of it immediately. More and more the boy next to him stiffened in the excitement. At one climactic point in the speech he shouted something Nihar could not understand, but it was immediately taken up by all the group. This all seemed real. It was alive. Something was being born here. He, too, would like to belong.

Yet he was glad when Nanda finally motioned to him to go out. Vinod and he took her to a tram. Nihar felt awkward when he found himself alone with Vinod. Nanda shielded him somehow, but Vinod was sharp and piercing. Was he afraid of Vinod? He seemed so positive, so sure of himself, so much the man who knew just where he was going.

They walked on together to Wellington Square. Vinod bought a few *bajjia*—the pretzel-like, sticky sweets that are a favorite of all young people in India—and they walked on to the little park to eat them. It was completely dark. Figures were lying on the grass, and the park was quiet except for the boy who made the rounds asking if they wanted a massage. Someday, Nihar thought, I will get courage enough to have a massage. But now Vinod had told him he would explain the purpose of the meeting, and Nihar was a ready listener.

Eleven o'clock, twelve, and then one. Still Vinod talked.

41

About the Revolution, about the U.S.S.R., about the rising masses, the deception of religion, and the treachery of the capitalistic West! He campaigned vocally against America, cursed the slavery of the government that had been sucked in by aid, and ended by telling Nihar that salvation lay with Marx. He promised to give Nihar some books that would tell him about all these things.

Vinod got up from the grass first. The city had become still. The night sky was filled with stars, and an old moon had come up sufficiently to give the whole place a pale, unreal appearance. Nihar was about to say good night when Vinod suggested that they walk over to his place, they could both stay there. In a few hours they would have to leave for the mill. So they walked, Vinod still talking, until they were back again at the club.

To call this a "place," thought Nihar, was somewhat of an exaggeration. The room where the meeting had been held had a court in which many of the comrades slept. It was here that Nihar slept that night, sharing Vinod's blanket. They lay close together, and for the first time in Calcutta Nihar could not go to sleep. His companion, however, was soon asleep.

What a strange person Vinod was! Not unfriendly, not unlikable, but impersonal! During the entire evening he had shown no evidence of affection, no particular concern. The talk had been a lesson, a long protracted lecture, and Nihar had been the pupil. He had interrupted only rarely to ask a question. Most of what had been said Nihar did not understand. He merely felt it must be right. The last thing that Vinod had said as they lay together was, "Nanda belongs! She's a regular if there ever was one. Get to know her better, and you'll see. She's all right." As he went to sleep, Nihar smiled as he thought about the vote he had cast in the first election. He did not tell Vinod about this. The next night Nihar brought his mat and his small box down to the hall and placed them next to Vinod's. He would belong. He would also talk to Nanda.

CHAPTER 5

Talking to nanda proved to be easier than he had expected. During the rest period one morning, she sought him out, apparently eager to find someone with whom she could talk. At first Nihar wondered at this because she knew Vinod so well.

"You enjoy talking to Vinod, don't you?" he had asked early in their acquaintance.

"Yes, when I want to talk politics. But talking to Vin is like talking to a salesman on duty. You always talk about his wares. What's more," she went on, "there's no time off for Vin. He never forgets he's got to start the Revolution. I've never caught him off duty. I met him on duty and that's how it has always remained."

"How long have you known him?" Nihar asked, innocent of the listening role he might fill in her life but flattered to think that a girl wanted to talk to him.

"I met him at the Young Communists' League. I live with my aunt and uncle, they've lived in Calcutta a long time." She stopped talking, looked furtively at Nihar. She seemed to be questioning whether she should go on, whether, perhaps, it was safe. She saw a strange, appealing smile come over the innocent face of a boy who was saying all over himself, "Please go on!"

"My uncle is a Party member," she continued. "But he never talks about politics at home. One day, however, there was a youth meeting, and he suggested that I might go with some of the office girls at the mill. I went, and it was during the meeting that I met Vinod. The program began with such a clamor of shouting slogans that I was deafened by the noise. That's what I like about the Communists, they all seem so alive."

Nihar wanted to break in to say that never in his life had he seen a girl so alive. The truth was that never before had he talked to a girl. He had just never had the opportunity. Were they all so alive? He couldn't remember any girl like this one in his village.

"What I don't like about the Communists," Nanda went on, "is their love of long speeches. I guess I must have shown all over my face that I couldn't understand any of the Bengali that was bursting forth. At least I do know that a boy sitting just to the side of me asked me in English if I could understand. I didn't answer directly. I just registered consternation, and he began to tell me what was being said. It's the only evidence of real concern I've ever seen in Vin."

"Vinod does understand the people here at the mill, doesn't he?" Nihar asked.

"Understand them? Well, yes and no. He understands the miserable condition in which they live. He knows that under the present regime there'll not be a change."

44

Other days they talked about the workers. Nanda liked them, she even confessed that she liked the noise of the mill. As she hurried to work in the early hours of the morning with her uncle, she felt driven on by a necessity that she could not understand. It seemed to accelerate the slow movements of the strange conglomeration of five thousand chattering human beings who crowded into the mill gate and ran through the darkness to the sections where they worked. The strange necessity that drove them was the fear of hunger and poverty. They were the fortunate people who had work, the especially fortunate people employed in this mill where the Scottish owners had been considerate of the needs of the workers and where, out of good business sense perhaps, the owners had provided intelligent labor officers and doctors and sanitary facilities better than those in most mills in India. Nanda's first contact in the mill, she told Nihar, had been with the lady labor officer who had interviewed her and had accepted her as an extra worker.

So many of the people she met were extras. They filled in in the various departments when the regulars were absent or went on leave. She learned very soon that leave was the great event of the year. Eight weeks were allowed each year, eight weeks during which the men could go back to their villages to see their wives and become acquainted again with their children whom they had not seen, perhaps, for ten months or a year. Eight weeks during which they were again family men at leisure to be waited upon by their women, to sit for long hours with the less traveled village men and tell stories about the big city, the mill, the life outside and beyond the little road of the village. Eight weeks to enjoy the cooking of a woman who was skilled

45

in making *chapatties*, the flat, flabby bread that was the limp companion to all meals, and varieties of curries. Eight weeks during which bickering went on for buying a small piece of land, a new plow, or a bullock with the money that had been saved up in the city. Eight weeks to help on the repair of the home to make it safe against the monsoon rains. Eight weeks, more often than not, spent in trying to get a deal with a moneylender so that part of the family debt could be liquidated or a dowry arranged for one of the daughters of the family or, most fortunate of all, some new jewelry—bright silver bracelets, heavy necklaces, nose rings, earrings, or anklets—could be bought. Eight weeks away from the coolie lines where the men lived on the mill property, ten to twelve in one room, away from the smoke, smells, and heat that dulled all senses so that they became dormant until awakened once a year by the clean but dusty smell of the countryside. Eight weeks to be spent among decent women, out of the company of men and their ubiquitous stories of manly feats, their tall tales of masculine conquest, and the nauseating dirtiness of their experience. Eight weeks of living again toward the time of return when the oldest boy or girl might go back with the father to the mill and the family income might be increased by amounts that seemed fabulous to the impecunious villager.

Nanda did not have this expectancy of release with which the workers lived from year to year. She only knew that some women she met had also received leaves, six weeks for the later pregnancy period and confinement time. They did not go back to their native places, most of them. They had time off for babies born in the filth and dirtiness of

Calcutta, slum babies who were more fortunate than many in the city because they could soon be brought to the *crèche* at the mill and kept there while their mothers worked. There they would receive good care and milk. When they were sick, they would be given treatment that their parents could never ordinarily afford.

Nanda filled in until her turn came to be put into the regulars. She had not been at the mill long before she learned a little Bengali and was drawn into the chitchat or listened to the idle gossip of the coolie women as they talked of petty scandals and of incidents that were told with so much relish that Nanda knew they were expressive of wishes that would never be fulfilled. Many of the workers were poor, ugly, often physically repulsive girls and women venting their frustrations through the malicious gossip that was always centered on the more attractive girls.

Nanda confessed to Nihar that she missed the happy companionships of girls she had known in Kandy. Many of her leisure hours were spent writing letters to them, telling them about Calcutta, the mill, and the incidental nothings that made her letters as well as the replies from her friends interesting. There were innuendos and hints in Nanda's letters, mostly the creations of her own mind written to mystify her friends. But she discovered that when she wrote about the incident of seeing Nihar at the mill, the girls immediately replied, relating more wonderful experiences of their own. And before she was aware of it, she had spun a fabulous lot of incidents out of whole cloth, none of which were even remotely true. The letters were interesting, though.

Here in the midst of a huge city she was living in her

47

imagination. She dreamed, not of a country youth like Nihar, but of young men who were clerks in important offices, boys who had gone to college and who were preparing for exciting and interesting jobs with great business concerns, jobs that would take them to the places that were stamped on the bales of finished burlap sacks at the mill—places where she might go sometime and from which she might bring back trinkets and jewelry that could be seen in museums or in the bazaars in Banaras or the shops in the China Bazaar in Madras.

"You want to go back?" On this day Nihar was not conscious that his voice betrayed the reason for his question.

"Yes, Ceylon's wonderful. It's like a fairy isle. I wouldn't be here if I had not come up to Sarnath where Buddha delivered his first sermon after he became the Enlightened One. My father and I came on a pilgrimage with a lot of other people."

"And you stayed here?" Nihar interrupted.

"Not intentionally. After Sarnath we went to Benares, and in spite of the fact that one is not supposed to get sick after bathing in the Ganges, my father did have trouble. We came here immediately because his sister was here. He had always wanted to make the pilgrimage to Sarnath, and once he had done it, it just seemed as if his life ambition had been accomplished. He lived only a few weeks after that and died in Calcutta. I stayed on with my aunt because it was the simplest thing to do."

Nanda's story intrigued Nihar. This was his first contact with a girl, his first acquaintance with a Buddhist. At least he assumed she was a Buddhist, although he never quite got around to asking her. It had seemed a little too intimate at first, and she had never broached the matter. Now, he felt sure, she had a new religion in the zeal she showed for the Party. They must talk about that. Perhaps he could tell her he had voted for the Party, that he, too, had changed his allegiance.

CHAPTER 6

I USED TO BELIEVE THAT, too. I know better now. All religions are the same, they all lead to the same source. It doesn't make any difference whether it's Krishna, Buddha, Mohammed, or Jesus, they are all supposed to lead to the same God." Nanda had opened the conversation sooner than Nihar had expected as they talked one noon at the mill.

"They are all equally selfish," she went on. For the tenth time perhaps, she described some incident that showed conclusively that man's drives are all the same, that religion does not really affect them at all. She had nothing good to say about the missionaries in Ceylon.

"They're British or American first, and then Christians. Or I should have said that they are capitalists first and everything else after that."

"In my village there was a padre," Nihar started to protest. But Nanda was quick to stop his objection.

"Oh, I know, a god-fearing man who gave up everything to come to this godforsaken land, gave up everything except his comfortable living, his jeep, his hill station, and

49

his air-conditioned bungalow! Get wise, Nihar, to all this propaganda. The missionaries are nothing but the stooges of the government. Their schools and hospitals are all subsidized. They take their orders not from God but from the church. They are all the victims of the economic system of the people who send them out."

"You haven't seen the whole picture," Nihar ventured to suggest. "Their best work is in the villages, and you wouldn't know a village if you saw one. I grew up in one. I know what happened to my father when he tried to break through caste and become a carpenter."

That evening they walked down to a tank near the Victoria Memorial, a monument that had been the center of derisive comment by both Nanda and Vinod. Nihar had made up his mind that he knew Nanda well enough now to tell her about his father. When they reached the tank, they sat on the steps.

"When I was growing up, my father was a Jack-of-all-trades as well as a farmer," he began. "He mended plows and did little jobs of carpentry that were too insignificant for the carpenter of the village to do. He was not in debt like everybody else who tried to marry off a daughter or get a piece of land. Still, I don't think I can remember a time when we didn't need money. One day I heard my father talking to some of the other men. There was something in him that made him rebel against this slavery in which we lived."

"Right word," interrupted Nanda. "It was and is slavery, and the people will go on living this way until we overthrow the system that causes it."

"But my father made the change within the system, or I

guess you'd say he made the system change from within." Nihar was intent upon telling his story, and he began to gain confidence.

"There was a caste carpenter named Ram Singh in the village. He lived over on the other side from where we lived, naturally. One day my father got up earlier than usual. I was still in bed when I heard my mother questioning him about what he was going to do.

" 'I'm going to Ram Singh's,' he asserted. 'I'm going to ask him to let me learn the carpenter's trade.'

" 'And a lot of good that will do you,' I heard my mother saying as I came alive to a day that was to be different from any I had known.

" 'I've made up my mind,' Father said. 'I'm going. We can't keep on like this. If I could afford to buy the tools, I think I could be a good carpenter, and since there is more work now with these new houses in Pakaur, I'm going.'

"My mother knew that once he had made up his mind, there was no use trying to stop him. She had seen him talking with the other men of the village, and she had been aware of his troubled look as he brooded over the problems that faced him. My older brother had not been able to go to school. But I was the younger, and Father was fond of me. He used to say I was going to school, he had made up his mind to that. The only school was the missionary school at Pakaur.

"By the time all this talking had taken place that morning I had washed. I was only eight at the time, and I didn't know what most of this was all about. But I made up my mind to follow my father when he started off with one of the men who had been talking to him.

51

"Ram Singh, the carpenter, began work early. There were new houses to be built, and there were houses in the bazaar section of the town some distance away that needed repair. My father soon reached the carpenter's shop. He stood in the yard watching, as if to time his attack and to make it when it was most advantageous. Finally there came the moment when Ram Singh stopped to take *pan*. This was a moment of relaxation in the early coolness of the day, and it must be seized. Ram Singh had noticed a man watching him, but he had not been aware that it was my father. Village men often watched him at work, probably envious of the good tools this carpenter had. Ram Singh knew my father and respected him, for he had a reputation in the village for honesty and thrift.

" '*Salaam, Bhai,*' said my father, forcing himself to be forward enough to make himself known.

" '*Salaam,*' answered Ram Singh in an offhand way, perfunctory decency making him return the greeting of a low-caste man.

" 'I have come to ask something of you, *Bhai*, something that will help all of us to earn our living in a respectable manner.'

" '*Acha?*' The tone of his voice changed. In spite of his attempt at being disinterested, he showed his curiosity.

" 'Let me come here to help you. Let me learn carpentry so that I can teach others and we can help one another.'

"Ram Singh stood rigid, his face at first perplexed. Then the full meaning of what Father had said seemed to dawn on him.

" '*Sudra!* you—you—you have the nerve to ask me to teach you a trade that has been in my family for genera-

52

tions, that needs tools that are costly! What God has given you to do, you ought to do!'

"He was pleased with his own outburst, and this spurred him on to a still greater tirade.

" 'Why, why you . . . How dare you come here with this impertinence? The next thing you will be asking me to let you live with us. This cannot go on. It just goes to show that all decency, all sense of rightness is breaking down. I won't have it. I'll teach you to be impudent enough to come to me, you. . . .'

"And as his indignation mounted, Ram Singh seized the plank that he had been measuring, and before my father could dodge out of the way, he struck him squarely on the back. Disregarding the stinging pain, my father ran away, the carpenter close on his heels. The few men who were listening scattered as quickly as possible, not wishing to be implicated in this quarrel. I had managed to run around the crowd and was in front of my father when he stopped far down the road.

"In spite of his age, my father was agile. He easily outran Ram Singh, but not before the irate carpenter had shouted defiance at all the forces that were seeking to break down the old caste system and put an end to everything that was proper and right under the old way. For days the men told my father that Ram Singh fumed at his work, lecturing to all the men who stopped to watch him. What were we coming to anyway? These things were unheard of, and something must be done to put a stop to them. Yes, something must be done!

"I shall never forget the days that followed this incident. I was too young to know just what it meant, too young to know that it was the evidence of a change that was beginning. I only know that I made up my mind that I would learn to do something worth while for a living and that nobody would stop me."

Nanda was listening with genuine interest.

"And what happened? I suppose your father buckled under and thanked God for what he had!"

"Not my father," Nihar was quick to rise to his defense. "He was simply more determined than ever that something had to change. I think he made up his mind that he would learn a trade and that he would teach it to other members of his family. At least it was only about a year after this incident that I remember I was sitting under our large mango tree, holding an old sari that belonged to my mother. I was there to frighten the birds or monkeys who came to steal the fruit. I would yell at the top of my voice when the parakeets or monkeys got into the tree and then wave the sari. It was an endless job from dawn to darkness, but I didn't mind so much because I could play in between these attacks on the ripening mangoes.

"I was shouting at the top of my voice that morning when I saw some men coming down the road toward our place. There was a white man with them, a missionary sahib who had been in the village many times. My grandfather had first known the Christians. He raised his family to have respect for them and he himself became a Christian. This white man had given my father some ointment for the sore on his back where he had been struck by the plank.

"That morning they came directly to our house, and one of the men went to the back where my father was working on a rope machine that he had made at the missionary's suggestion and on which he had taught several of the men to make rope for the cattle. My father was glad to see this friend again, and he came quickly from the back yard.

"'I think you're going to be a carpenter,' said the missionary. 'I've brought a carpenter from Mysore side to teach you.'

"I had never paid too much attention to what was said in the many meetings my father had with the missionary. But what he said that morning I shall never forget because my father repeated it again and again whenever he told the story of how he became a carpenter and, what was even more important for us at that time, an active Christian worker.

"'Our God revealed his love through Jesus who became a carpenter,' the missionary said. 'Jesus learned the trade from Joseph, and the first thirty years of his life he spent in a carpenter's shop. He was a worker. While he cut and smoothed wood, he planned for the still greater work he was to do—to help men because they needed better houses and better tools and a better world where these would be possible for all men.'"

"Quite a sermon," interrupted Nanda, who was becoming restless under Nihar's barrage of words.

"But it wasn't only words," Nihar continued, a strange sense of compulsion making him go on with the story. "The missionary had brought a carpenter, and the fellow stayed with us. And the coming of this man marked the beginning of the change in my family and in the village. The stranger brought tools that were even better than Ram Singh's, and in a short time we had more work than we could take care of. My father learned, and he, in turn, taught two of my uncles. My older brother and I learned, too. The man from Mysore left, and our home became the carpenter's school for men and boys from villages around.

"The final day of real triumph came when one of Ram Singh's men came to tell my father that the old man wanted to see him. The rumor in the village was that Ram Singh was angry because the new carpenters were so much more skillful than he, because they finished work when they promised they would, and because they could be relied upon to use good, well seasoned wood.

"Ram Singh was in his yard when my father came up. Four years had passed since the day he had approached the old carpenter and had asked to learn the trade. Ram Singh motioned for my father to come in and, what is more, to sit down. He talked about the business, how he had heard about the skill and honesty of the Christians who were carpenters. He called his bearer, and soon tea was brought.

"As the two men were about to drink together, Ram Singh said, 'I'm too old now to keep on working as I have. I'd like to sell my tools and all this equipment that I've gathered here. I'd like you to have them.'

" 'But I don't think I have enough rupees now to buy all this,' my father replied.

" 'I know, I've thought of that. I'd like to make a bargain with you. We need a school here and equipment, slates and books and all the rest. I'll give the ground and the money for the wood, you figure what the work will cost and count that figure against the tools and worktables I have here. I don't want these tools to be idle. Tools were made for use. Is that a bargain?'

"My father was quick to see what this might mean.

56

" 'We'll make it a community project,' he said, 'and why not let all the village work on it? We'll do the carpentry and keep the building in repair. We can work together on something we all need.'

"I worked on the school—we all did—and within a few months we had the building and slates and all the rest. Ram Singh did not live long after that. One day just before he died, my father, as was his custom, went to see him.

" 'I've not forgotten what you said about your carpenter Jesus.' The old man's voice was weak and tired. 'I'd like this house to be his house. You Christians need a church. This house has been a carpenter's place. It can just keep on being that. I like a religion that works, that works because it believes in work. Keep it that way.' "

Nanda and Nihar sat watching the reflection of the Southern Cross in the tank. Neither of them said anything. Nihar looked from the reflection up to the sky. His mind went back to his father, to the cross that was made for the play. He wanted to tell Nanda about it, but he didn't. He knew he would one day and then Nanda might understand.

CHAPTER 7

NIHAR WAS NO LESS surprised than was Nanda at the protracted story he had told. It was the first time since he had come to Calcutta that he had talked in this way, with a sense of deep compulsion to tell his story. And now that he had done it, he felt uneasy. Suddenly the work he was doing at the mill became meaningless, or rather it became something wrong for him to do. He felt within him the old yearnings, the need for expression, and, above all, a longing for the sense of doing something that was worth while, as worth while as his father's carpenter shop and apprentice school.

If only he knew the right persons to talk to, if only he could plan with someone. Yes, that was it, someone who would understand the difference between the kind of planning he thought Vinod and Nanda were doing and what he wanted to do. This thought haunted him as he worked, even though it did not keep him from making rather good progress in the mill. He had gone from the batching department to the preparing, from this to the spinning and then to the winding. He had had no trouble at the mill. The incessant noise and the dust had filled his senses so that he had become unfeeling as long as he was in the mill compound.

Nihar did not see Nanda for several days after their long evening together. Then one day he passed her as she was leaving in the afternoon, and she told him that she had been sick.

"I've got to go home tonight," she said impersonally, "but I have been wanting to see you. I wrote out something in a little book that I suppose was meant to be a stupid autograph book, and I want you to have it."

Nanda pulled down the strap of her shoulder bag with its bright embroidery and fumbled in it for a moment. Out came a pocket edition of a book, then her pen and a handkerchief, and finally a little black notebook. Nihar remembered the night they had wandered along Chawringi Road and had stopped at a litter of notebooks spilled on a white sheet on the sidewalk. Nanda had bargained for two of them, and Vinod had joked with her about getting autographs.

"You ought to get B. C. Roy's," he had said. "It will be the last signature of the old order."

"I want nothing less than Nehru's," Nanda had said in mock seriousness.

Here was the little black book again. Nanda handed it to Nihar and waved a good-by. She was strange, this girl, stranger than anyone he had ever known. He had an intuitive feeling that so much that she said she didn't really believe, that she was talking herself into an attitude, that she was continuously arguing herself into a position. She was defensive, rather unnecessarily so, he felt, but he did not know why. Perhaps, he thought, that is the way Buddhists are! Or is it because she is Ceylonese? Both were a mystery to him.

Without opening the book, he put it into his pants pocket, jumped on a bus, and started for the room that Vinod and he had now taken together. It was a small, back room at the top of an old business block. The room was empty except for the stacks of books and magazines that Vinod had and the two steel trunks they had both bought in a burst of extravagance so they could keep their treasures and their money locked up. For Nihar his trunk had become his savings bank. For Vinod his was the secret place to hide the most precious literature from the U.S.S.R. What a man locks up, he had said, indicates his standard of values.

Vinod spent most of his evenings at meetings or talking with groups of men whom Nihar found difficult to like.

59

They were all so intense, so preoccupied, so impersonal. Again and again he had come back to the room, hoping that Vinod would be there so that they might do something together or just talk, not about abstract social theory, but about people and how one felt. Most of the time Vinod was not there.

His lack of friends had driven Nihar more and more to the books that Vinod collected. He had often taken one up to Wellington Square where he would sit on the grass reading until it was too dark to see. Then if he could find Vinod or some of the other men, he would eat at a hotel where he could get his evening meal for a remarkably low price. He had taken to talking to the boys he met there, but for the most part they were not interested in anything but sports or movies, and they seemed to divide their time between these. The fellows were often the ones he had seen practicing on the bars or lifting the weights in the gym schools in the park. They had looked interesting then, but their glamour faded when they put on their clothes. All they read were physical culture magazines from England or America and Indian movie magazines.

On this particular evening when he did not find Vinod in their room, Nihar did not pick up the book he had been reading. His hand felt the little bump in his pants' pocket that he knew was the book Nanda had given him. He took a hasty bath, a ritual he did not usually like to hurry after a day at the mill, and put on clean pants and a bush shirt. That was always the sign of a celebration. He then started for the park, his hand holding the book in his pocket as he hurried along the street. He always liked to save the few letters that he got to read until the proper time. It was the same with this book. He must find just the right place, and then he would read.

Nihar walked around the little park, recognizing one or two of the familiar figures who frequented the place in the evening. He stopped to watch a young teacher or sadhu, naked except for a loincloth. His long black hair hung to his shoulders, and he was reciting some portions of the Gita. Then very much as a dog might walk around and around a spot to lie down, Nihar circled a little plot of grass and finally settled, his handkerchief serving as protection for his pants.

Not until he was seated did he take the book out of his pocket. He put it down on the grass in front of him and then looked around as if to make sure no one was within seeing distance. He was ready to read what Nanda had written. As he turned the cover, he found an inscription:

> For Nihar after our discussion
> on life and religion,
> Nanda

And in a corner had been written the date, October 16, 1952. On the next page in neat yet distinctly personal script, he read:

For you: I have given up believing in God. I have found something real to believe in. I believe in man. You must believe in man, you must believe in yourself. Live for people, and they will make you live forever. Though full of miseries and trouble, this life is worth living. Do not try to seek escape from this, struggle hard to make this life happy for all.

But only wishing is not the end. Our struggle must be based on the realization of life. Today there is one reality common throughout the world. There are, for example, many people who suffer from starvation and oppression while others exploit and oppress their fellow men.

This state of affairs is so general and widespread that people have begun to take it for granted. You may call it destiny, but I call it ignorance. Let the capitalists of India, like Tata and Birla, suck the blood of the millions and millions of our country, and you call it destiny. Let the Americans, British, and French exploit the Asians and keep them slaves, and call it destiny.

But if this is destiny, then I tell you the rising masses of the world are struggling hard to take this fate in their own hands. Come out of the world of pessimism and see a new sun rising in the East. A new world is being born. Ignorance is the greatest sin, and you keep yourself ignorant of the fast-changing world. Like the youth of other countries, why do you not align yourself with the masses in the struggle against capitalism and imperialism?

The days of religion are gone. Religion cannot solve a single problem of life in the present world of materialism. It is a means of propaganda in the hands of capitalists to exploit the minds of innocent people. Like the detective novels and pictures, religious books are the stories of the past world and give you nothing but pessimism, sometimes almost persuade you to commit suicide. They preach to you to hate this life, and you dream of paradise. Make this world paradise. There is no other world than this though it is a hell at present.

Man is not on this earth only to be happy, he is not here simply to be honest. He is here to realize great things for humanity and to attain nobility.

Eagerly Nihar turned the page. Surely there was something more, something for him, a boy. Something from Nanda, a girl, a human being, for him. But the next page was blank, and the next and the next. All the rest!

As the book slipped out of his hands onto the grass, he did not notice that a little note fell out of it. Tears came to his eyes. He covered his forehead with the palms of his hands and gradually slid them down over his face. He sobbed and felt somewhat relieved. Then he suddenly became resentful.

What he wanted was not a political treatise, he wanted a declaration of friendship. What he wanted was some little concern from Nanda, from Vinod, for him as a person. He felt he could not stand these sermons and chewed-over lectures that came from books. He felt sure Nanda had copied this from some tract. It was all so frightening. If only he could go back to Bihar, he would never come back to this city again. If only . . . but he could not think it out. He felt too deeply. He was too lonely. One cannot think when one is lonely.

How long he sat in this mood he did not know. He was oblivious to all that went on around him. It had become dark. He was completely startled when a very large fireworks fountain cascaded just back of him, the sparks from it falling all around him, even on the little black book. At first he felt inclined just to let the book stay there, yet he knew it would not burn. It would just be propaganda for someone else to read. So he reached down to pick it up only to see the folded paper that had fallen out of it. A spark had burnt a hole through it.

His anticipation came back, and with expectancy he picked it up. Of course, she would not write personally in the book. Who would in an autograph book? She had chosen to write a personal note, that was it. How stupid of him not to understand. He could not wait to read it. He had scarcely walked out of the way of another fireworks fountain when he opened it.

Nihar:

I have taken a lot of time to write these pages in the book I want you to have. What I have said, think over. I'm not preaching to you. I'm just trying to tell you to wake up. I've been awake now for about a year. You would have liked me in Ceylon before that. I was everything you Indians think a girl should be—demure, sweet, and dumb. I'm grateful to my uncle and to Vinod for awakening me. I'd like to see you wake up, too. I won't see you again for a while. I'm leaving tomorrow for Ceylon. My aunt must go home on family matters, and she's offered to take me with her. So I'm going. I don't know when I'm coming back, but I will come back. Take care of Vinod for me and say good-by to him for me. He would not like a note, it would be sentimental! And remember, Comrade, I will write to you, and when I do, you must write back. Please! You're so nice, so unspoiled, so waiting to be spoiled! Wait until I come back before you are ruined.

Yours,
Nanda.

P.S. Read what I have written in the book five times each day for the next week. Let that be your daily devotion! This is a prescription.

P.P.S. I'll write to you in care of Vinod. This will irritate him, and you will know he's human.

Nihar's first impulse was to go to her home. "Take care of Vinod." "So waiting to be spoiled," he said out loud to himself, and he grew hot and angry all over. He crumpled the note in his hand and was about to throw it away when he thought better of it. He put it in his pocket along with the book. He was hungry. He would have some food, or was that spoiling himself? For Nanda of all people to say that! She was not capable of spoiling anyone. She'd be a much better person if she were!

When he got to the edge of the park, he could not get across the street. A Kali celebration was passing. Auto lorries carried huge statues of the black Kali, the goddess of destruction, standing in her familiar pose, in one of her hands a knife that she had just used to cut off the head of one of her victims. It was dripping blood. She held the bleeding head in the other hand while she stood with her foot on the headless body. She wore a string of human heads around her neck. The organization sponsoring this truck had also put garlands of jasmine and marigolds around her neck. There were fruits and sweets and incenses at her feet and a band in tawdry gay uniform walking in front. An elephant, too! Then came boys exploding fireworks, still more fireworks fountains, statues in cycle rickshaws, red lights, torches, Petromax lanterns carried high above the heads of coolies who walked at the sides of trucks that bore still more of the same statues, statues of Kali killing people, Kali decorated, Kali receiving rose petals and the *puja* of people who wished to escape her vengeance and destruction. Lights, noise, a kind of music, racket, people!

Nihar stood watching. He was fascinated by it all. He had never seen celebrations this elaborate in his village. The whole city was in carnival mood. The loud-speaker on the corner screeched with the tune of one song that was played again and again. This was all part of Calcutta, part of the surprise and endless change in this amazing city. Riots, elections, festivals, all came and went in the pattern of living in Calcutta. Each seemed to belong. For most of the settled population, these did not matter. But for the sidewalk dwellers and the students, it was the excitement that kept life interesting.

Suddenly without knowing exactly why, Nihar, too, felt wild and mad. He would like to have danced with the boys in front of the idol as he used to dance at district school festivals held in Pakaur. He wanted to follow the procession to the tank where the statue would be immersed. He would give himself to this simple popular religion. At the same time he felt he ought to rush in front of the parade, shout slogans at it, and call it superstitious and ignorant. He felt a sudden, sick feeling in the pit of his stomach, as if he were going to vomit.

He must get away. He must go home. Nanda was going home, he would go, too. He would leave the mill. If he never made any more money, what difference did it make? He must get away!

CHAPTER 8

NIHAR MIGHT HAVE escaped had he not gone to his room that night. The din of the music, the shooting crackers, and the yelling still in his ears, he turned back to the little attic room where he hoped he would find Vinod. He must talk to someone, and Vinod would be better than no one. How strange it is, he thought as he walked faster and faster down the rapidly clearing streets with the shrouded bodies of boys and men stretched out on the sidewalk asleep, how strange that I should be running away from Calcutta. He had run away from his village to come to the city. He had found Nanda and Vinod and Communism, but he had not found satisfaction. He had not found himself.

Vinod was in the room. Nihar could see the light before he climbed the dark steps. And as he got nearer to the door, he heard a voice, but it was not speaking in the series of intense, short noises that he had come to associate with Vinod. He stopped, dismayed that anyone else should be there. Another one of the gang, he concluded, which meant talk, until morning perhaps, about the evils of Congress men or about some fantastic idea like those they had sometimes discussed until the first streaks of dawn sent Nihar out to take a bath. Endless talk, talk, talk, the token of modern India, the curse of the country!

He would go back to the park again. He just could not face a night of talk. And yet he wanted to have a certain kind of talk, he wanted to tell someone, anyone, that he was fleeing from this city, from all that it had meant when he saw the Kali worship. He was getting out! As he stopped on the narrow stairs halfway up, he heard someone come to the top of the landing.

"Hi!" It was Vinod who had heard him coming. There was no escape. The light of the electric bulb hit his face.

"Well, what's the humanitarian been up to tonight? Come, confess, where have you been?" Nihar was accustomed to Vinod's teasing about his ramblings and his increasing unconcern for social and political theories.

"Why so glum? Nanda been nasty to you, my boy?" Nihar was in no mood for this.

"Please, Vinod, not tonight! I'm for bed."

"Then come into the canopied splendor of this boudoir. I'll get my lackeys to help you off with your cumbersome clothes!" Nihar had not seen Vinod in this mood for a long time. He must have had an advance at the mill. Or had he been made an officer in the club?

"I'm for bed, I said, and the quicker the better." As Nihar pushed his roommate aside, he saw the person whose voice he had heard. He stopped, not because he was not used to finding boys in the room with Vinod, but because the one he saw this night startled him. He was dressed in a *khadi* or homespun dhoti with a gray-brown shawl over his bare shoulders. His face was different, Nihar couldn't quite decide why, and his long hair might have been the badge of a sadhu. He was not particularly distracted by Nihar's entrance. He merely looked up, and a faint smile came to his lips.

"This is Talat," said Vinod. "He's just come to Calcutta from Chandil to see B. C. Roy. This is Nihar, Talat, our dreamer who's waiting for Christ to come again."

This remark probed Nihar awake.

"And I suppose you have gotten well acquainted with Vinod. He's waiting for Lenin to rise from the dead and come in glory to the poor downtrodden masses of India."

"Precisely, precisely, my boy! You're part of the mass, my beloved, you're part of it!"

Nihar had suddenly lost his desire to go to bed, not because Vinod had been sarcastic, but because he had taken a closer look at the stranger. Nihar was aware of him suddenly, as one is sometimes conscious of a person whom one may not even see—something about him, something more

68

than just a physical presence, something that makes one aware of another. Yes, that was it, a sense of awareness seemed to be stirred by the visitor.

"Did I hear you correctly? You've come to see Dr. B. C. Roy? What for?" Nihar was genuinely curious.

"Vinoba Bhave has malignant malaria, and Talat has come to check up on the arrangements for Roy to go to him." Vinod was patronizingly eager to explain.

Nihar was confused and amazed. Bhave? Yes, he knew about him. He had heard quite a lot of talk about him. But he could not remember just what except that the Communists had made fun of him for trying to collect land from the landowners to give it to the landless, to stave off the Revolution, they said. Part of his confusion was also due to the name of this strange boy—Talat. Surely that was a Muslim name. He did know enough about Bhave to know that he was a *pucka* or pure Hindu and that his movement had roots in Hinduism.

"I'm just a *yatrik*, a pilgrim," the boy volunteered. "I've joined what is called the Bhoodan Yajna movement. I'm a Muslim."

"Chance acquaintance," interrupted Vinod. "I was coming back from having some food. I missed you tonight, Nihar, didn't you eat?" Vinod often asked questions that might have led to personal conversations, but he never waited for an answer. There are always more important things to talk about than mere personal problems, Nihar had been told again and again as Vinod had counseled him to drown these in the larger concerns, the big problems of the social order! He was in the midst of this thought when Vinod went on.

69

"Talat was trying to find Roy's house, and he got held up by death and destruction on parade tonight, so we got to talking in Wellington Square. I've been wanting to talk with someone about Vinoba, so I asked Talat to stay with us tonight."

Nihar was both irritated and fascinated. As he spread his mat on the floor, he hoped that Talat would be next to him. He saw he could maneuver this because their guest had few possessions and no sleeping bag. Nihar offered him half of his mat, and the two of them stretched out. Vinod turned off the light. There had been conversation about the Kali celebrations, nothing about Bhoodan or about Talat himself. Talat was obviously worn out, and he wanted to sleep. When Nihar thought that both boys had settled down, he decided he must tell Vinod about his decision to go home.

"I'm quitting the mill tomorrow," he began. "I'm going home."

"Home?" Vinod's voice at once showed his surprise as well as his disgust. "Home to what?"

"Cut it, Vinod. I'm not in the humor tonight. I'm fed up, and I want to go somewhere to think things through."

"You certainly have chosen the right place. Go to the village, young man! That's what all the speakers say at convocations. Go to the village, the heart of this great country, any one of the six hundred thousand of them, and build bore-hole latrines and compost pits and the kingdom will be just around the corner!"

Nihar decided he could stop this tirade, which was only a variation of one he had heard over and over from Vinod. He would stop this ranting once and for all.

70

"I've got a message for you. Want to hear it?"

"Must I?" asked Vinod in the midst of a yawn.

"Nanda's going back to Ceylon." Nihar waited. If anything could waken an emotion, any feeling for a person in Vinod, surely this would.

"Think I'll go along. I'd like to meet her mother for an obvious reason. When?"

Nihar wanted to pounce on him, beat him, beat him until he cried for mercy. Instead he thought he would torture him with the answer.

"I think she may have gone already. She sent me a note. In fact, she gave me a book in which she wrote a farewell."

Vinod yawned again. "Too bad. She's a good girl, and she's on her way to being a good Party member. I must keep track of her."

Nihar was furious. Such thick-skinned indifference! He hated it. Party or no Party, Nanda was a person first. She was a girl. These Communists! Then he felt slightly amused. He remembered quickly a vote dropped in a box on election day and big talk at meetings where he had poohpoohed most of his former ideas and had been led along to agreement that Revolution was on the way.

He stretched out, the relaxed body of Talat next to his, too close in the warm Calcutta night. He was not sleepy now. He would like to talk to this boy next to him who was so calm and composed, so relaxed and peaceful. How does one get that way, he thought. How can one be that way in the midst of a world like this?

The distant jangle of bands in Kali processions could still be heard. Nihar tried to compose himself, wishing at the same time that he could see Talat's face. But Talat must be asleep. So he lay quiet, his face turned toward their guest.

"Do you really want to go home?" a low voice said almost in a whisper.

Nihar did not move. This was Talat speaking. He was not asleep. Nihar put his hand out as if to reach for something to take hold of. Talat sensed the movement and lifted his head.

"Why don't you come back to Chandil with me?" That was all he said. But he touched Nihar's hand, and for the first time in Calcutta Nihar felt a warm, personal relationship.

Outside the music would sound nearer as the bands passed up the street. Then it would die away again as they disappeared in the direction of the tanks where the idols were to be dumped. How long he lay there thinking he wasn't sure, but the more he thought of it, the more he felt that it was not family nor the village he wanted. It was something more, something as real as the touch of a hand when it came from someone who had found home because he had found something real to live for. In one touch he had felt it, had known it was different. Vinod also had something to live for but something that had no place in it for the touch of a hand, the understanding of the heart, or respect for the individual. Vinod's was something that was ruthless, impersonal, and devastating. It was from this that he must flee. He must find a hand to hold in the companionship of working together for something he did not quite comprehend, something he vaguely thought meant the kindly, human way leading ultimately to peace and understanding.

72

CHAPTER 9

Vinod got up early. He seemed to have an inexhaustible supply of energy. He was always the last to bed and the first to get up in the morning. Something seemed to impel him, something that was as inexplainable as his lack of personal relationship and yet as dynamic as the force of something to live for.

"Are you really serious about quitting? Have you become a capitalist?" was all Vinod had said as he left. Nihar had merely turned over, pretending to be asleep. He had subconsciously hoped that Vinod would press him for an answer, be concerned because he was not going to the mill, or offer to see him later in the day. But this was like many other mornings when he had watched Vinod get up, take out a clean pair of shorts, pants, and a shirt, and start for his bath. So many mornings he had wanted him to suggest going to the cinema in the evening or just having food together or going to an exposition. He had even wished Vinod would invite him to the club, a place he had learned to dislike without really knowing why. It was always a meeting somewhere to which he was invited, always a speech and a discussion. Always there was the cold, analytical talk in which the men harangued about the masses but never seemed to talk about people. They always talked about the Revolution but never seemed to be aware of the suffering on the sidewalks or the tragedy that lay exposed on the thresholds of houses.

Something inside Nihar wanted to rise up this morning

to stop Vinod—something as stark and naked as his soul, as pitiful and needy. Nihar wanted, without knowing it, to confront Vinod as a person, to ask him for brotherhood instead of political comradeship, for concern rather than condemnation, for warmth and affection rather than cold aloofness and intellectual agreement.

When he heard sandals patter on the pavement outside, Nihar knew Vinod was gone. He had never really seemed to be there except in a vague ideological way. Nihar now had a chance to look at the stranger who had come the night before, the stranger whom Vinod had invited up to talk and who now was suddenly abandoned by Vinod, left to the kindlier care of Nihar.

Talat's body was half uncovered when Nihar looked at him. His long hair had fallen over his face. His wheat-colored skin was firm over muscles that had been trained in the outdoors. He must be about their age. Strangely enough, Nihar felt a sense of relationship to him that he could not explain. He sat looking at him. Talat, as if sensing this, raised his arm and shoved the curly hair back over his forehead. His face was small, his eyes light brown, and his half beard somewhat straggly on his cheeks and chin. Nihar noticed his well formed shoulders and the firmness of his legs.

"Are you waiting for me to go?" the stranger asked.

"Not at all," Nihar was quick to answer. "Must you go right away?"

Talat smiled. It was not the derisive smile, the sneer to which Nihar had become accustomed. It was suggestive of friendliness, the expression of a bond, the avenue to relationship.

74

"I'm not going back to the mill," continued Nihar. "I'll leave a note with Vinod. I'm really going home."

The next fifteen minutes the boys did not get up. Nihar told Talat about the mill. He told him about Vinod, about the Party, about the organizing that Vinod had done, about how he had been a part of it as someone on the fringe. He became rather enthusiastic about this subject, and for a few moments he pictured a rather exciting and interesting life to his new friend.

"Then you're a Communist?" asked Talat, a slight inflection in his voice that might be interpreted as disappointment.

"I voted Communist," Nihar explained, "like thousands of others because I didn't know any other way. Something's got to be done, and at least the Communists are serious about it, at least they have a program."

It was the first time that Nihar had said anything like this out loud.

"Do you know the land-gift movement, the Bhoodan Yajna?" asked Talat.

"Oh, I've read about it, and I've admired Vinoba. But I guess I've listened to Vinod's scorn of it too long. He admires Vinoba, but he thinks the whole idea of giving up land by those who have it to those who don't is a silly dream or, what is more likely, a device to capture the minds of people so that they will not support the Revolution that will change the whole economic system."

"Yes, I know," Talat said sadly, "only Vinoba's revolution—for that is what it is—is much more thoroughgoing than anything the Communists are talking about. His revolution is threefold. He wants to change the hearts of people,

75

he wants to create a change in their lives, and he wants to change the social structure. He believes that nothing can be achieved through pressure or force."

Talat stopped and looked directly at Nihar. "Vinod said you used to be a Christian. You ought to feel a kinship with what Vinobaji wants. After all, it's what Jesus preached."

Talat's words struck Nihar in a most vulnerable spot. He felt wounded, as if he had been stabbed. He did not reply directly to this question.

"Another Gandhiji come to judgment!" Talat went on. "The most important thing that has happened in India since Gandhiji's death."

Nihar felt strangely awake, as if something that had slept a long time within him had been aroused. Something was stretching within him, trying to come to life. It was a different morning.

"I joined the movement in Bombay State when Bhave was not along. I . . ." Talat hesitated, then smiled and went on. "I am a Muslim, the first to join the pilgrims and to walk with Vinobaji, I think. I left Karachi just a year ago, went to Ceylon, and expected to go back to Pakistan by way of India on the pretext of some business for my uncle who lives in Lahore. I'm on my way back now, but I don't expect to get where I was going. I can't now, something's happened to me."

Nihar was fascinated. He had never heard anyone talk like this. This was what he had been waiting for. Here was someone alive to an importance in living, to an ideal to which he was devoted. Yet here, too, was someone who seemed to be concerned, who had a warmth and a joy that was personal not political.

76

"You must tell me all about it," Nihar said enthusiastically. "I want to know about it."

Talat had gotten up. "Let's have a bath. Where can we go?"

Nihar felt embarrassed. There was no place here that he could take Talat. But he had a sudden inspiration. He simply told Talat to wait a moment. He pulled his dhoti tight around his waist, and without bothering to cover the upper part of his body, he dashed out. Talat began to examine the room, his attention taken up with the stacks of books in the corner, the propaganda literature that Vinod had brought home and that he gave out to the eager boys who came to ask for it.

In a few minutes Nihar returned. He was delightfully excited, more alive than he had been for longer than he could remember.

"I asked the *memsahib* next door at the school if we could take a bath there. It's a Christian school, and they have nice bathing arrangements. I've talked to some of the teachers. They've invited me over, but I haven't gone because Vinod made fun of them. It's Durga Puja holidays, you know, and the students are not there. Come along!"

Talat took a clean loincloth out of the little bundle he had brought and a *khadi* dhoti, a white one, Nihar noticed, not the customary colored garment that Muslims wore. Talat did not have a shirt, or if he did, he did not bother to wear it.

"I'd like to wash some things, if I can," he said as he picked up his soiled clothes and started out.

Talat scrubbed his legs and feet, and Nihar dabbled in the water to mark time. Bathing can be a joy, Nihar thought. He always enjoyed it. It could also be a ceremony, and this morning he understood something of the significance that older Indians gave to it. Not once but again and again he poured the water over his head and body until his skin glistened even in the semidarkness of the room. He stretched, rubbed, and swished as he watched Talat. What a fine body he had, lean and supple, hardened by the walking he had done!

The washing with its accompanying inspection had to end. As the final buckets of water were slushed over their bodies, the boys enjoyed in this bathroom the luxury of a privacy that was not experienced in the street. Talat squashed his dirty clothes, pounded them for good measure, and then wrung them out. Nihar put on his clean fresh pants, and Talat fastened his dhoti.

"Where can I dry these?" He was laughing.

"Let's take them back to the room. We'll hang them out of the window," answered Nihar as they ran back to the room. That meant that Talat would have to come back to get them.

"I've got to get over to B. C. Roy's house soon," Talat said as they hung the washing out of the window. "I think I told you last night that Vinoba is sick, sicker than he will admit, and I've come to Calcutta to check on the plans for getting Roy out to Chandil. Atulya Ghosh is going with him." Nihar had seen Ghosh at various Congress rallies. "They're going to fly to Jamshedpur. Perhaps you had not heard that Rajendra Prasad is also to be there."

Nihar was impressed. India's president and top rank officials were going to Chandil! This little man was important. As the boys had their morning tea, they talked longer than Talat had expected. Nihar heard that the Acharya, a Hindu title meaning preceptor, or learned person, followed the Gandhian way of life and even bore a physical resemblance to the Mahatma. He cared little for his own life. This little caring was his best protection. At fifty-eight he had walked over eighteen hundred miles through five states, asking for free gifts from those who had land to give to the many impoverished tenants and landless laborers who needed it.

The talk might have gone on indefinitely had not Talat said again that he must go to Dr. Roy. As he started to go, he took Nihar's hand. "I'll come back for my things in an hour. I must start back this afternoon. Why don't you come with me?"

Nihar did not answer. He smiled, said a pleasant good-by, walked rapidly back to the room, unlocked his box, and counted his money.

CHAPTER 10

HE HAD SEVENTY RUPEES, more money than he had ever had before. He had meant to send it home where he knew his father would keep it for him. In fact, he had meant to take it to the post office the day before, but he had remembered that it was a holiday and the money order window would not be open. He had not written home for a long time. He must write this morning.

He took the little pad of writing paper that he had bought from the street vendor and began to write in Hindi:

I am going to Bihar, but I am not coming home. I have met a boy who is a disciple of Acharya Vinoba Bhave, and I am going to Chandil with him. Bhave has malaria, and he will not take drugs. But the pressure from all the leaders, even Rajendra Prasad, has been so strong that he has now agreed to accept medical aid. I may come home after I have been to Chandil. I will let you know. I will leave my address here with Vinod.

With love and prayers,
Nihar

He always signed his letters "with love and prayers." He didn't know why except that when his boyhood friend, Mohanlal, went off to the missionary school, he wrote to Nihar once and signed the letter in this way. This morning Nihar looked at what he had written. He could not help but smile as he read the words. He had made up his mind almost unconsciously on the spur of the moment, and this writing was the evidence of it, as if he needed to record the decision lest it be revoked. Strangely enough, however, he had a sense of the meaning of the words with which he had closed the letter. He did feel love for his father and his brothers, for the whole family, in fact. And just now, at this moment, he felt that prayer was real. He found himself sitting there on the floor on his mat being thankful. Something inside him was saying thanks for the boy who had come to the room the night before, for the mission in Calcutta on which he had been sent. As Nihar sat there, something more than thanks came into his consciousness. He did not say it out loud, but in the more real voice of his heart he found himself saying, "Please, God, let Vinobaji live. Please. . . ."

Nihar did not move for some time. He was inexpressibly happy. He had written home, but much more important, he had made connection again with something he had sought in faces of people on the street, in Nanda and in Vinod, but had not found. Now suddenly in a concern, a sincere desire, he had found a channel of communication that he did not understand but felt in every part of his being. It was as if he had made connection with a source of life from which he had been disconnected.

"Let Vinobaji live! O God, let me live, too. I'm not living now. . . . And thanks for sending Talat."

How easily and how naturally the words came! The paper on which the letter had been written fell from his knee. He reached down to pick it up, and his fingers touched the small embroidered bag that Talat had left on the floor beside the mat. Without thinking, at first, he picked it up and felt its contents. Just as he started to look inside, he heard someone on the stairs. He dropped the bag quickly, his guilty conscience making him push it farther from him. No one came into the room, and again Nihar took the bag in his hands. He could feel some small books and papers. Surely it was not wrong to look at the books.

His hand first felt a little volume which he took out of the bag. Because of the strange script that he could not recognize, he was unable to figure out what was written until he noticed in small print in parentheses on the title page the words, *The Holy Koran*. The book showed that it had been used. On some pages there were underlinings, and on most of them there were notes in a fine, neat script.

Nihar handled the book, held it awhile, and then put it down. It was a well read book. After he laid it down, he continued his search in the bag. Papers! Many of them and all sizes and shapes. On some there was writing in Hindi, and he could, without much difficulty, read these. He also saw some words in English. At first he hesitated, holding the papers loosely in his hand. He knew that he should not read them, that they were none of his business. The temptation, however, was too strong. He would just look, and if they were personal, he would put them back. He read:

"In everyone I see the image of God Himself."

"I am a humble servant with good will toward all. I have faith in the people."

"One way of redistributing land is by force and violence. Another is through nonviolence, and I am preparing the ground for the use of the peaceful method."

"I am only an instrument in the hands of him who is the Lord of all ages."

". . . the dedication of one's all for the well-being of all . . ."

". . . the age of Truth, Nonviolence, and Love has dawned upon us. You have a world to win and a way of winning it."

Nihar stopped reading, but these last words remained vividly in his mind. Then he continued to read:

"I have met a man who says he is not afraid to die, that God is his successor because the land belongs to God—the earth is the Lord's—and all we can do is serve the Lord. I will not go home until I have come to understand this man's greatness. I intend to become a disciple. . . ."

Nihar did not read further. He had seen the word "disciple," and in the cleanness of this morning, in the new life that he suddenly felt, the word was real. He kept saying to himself again and again, "I intend to become a disciple."

He gathered up the papers and, with the copy of the Koran, put them back into the bag. He must not read any more. The words might be too personal. He felt suddenly as if he were looking into someone's heart, into that person's innermost self, and that he had not asked permission. He would ask permission! That was friendship, asking permission to look into someone's heart!

When the bag had been shoved into the approximate place where he had found it, he picked up the writing pad again and wrote:

Vinod:
I am going to Chandil with Talat. I will let you know when I am coming back. Please notify the mill that I am taking leave from today. If a letter comes from Nanda, will you please send it to me at Vinoba Bhave's Camp, Chandil? I have paid my share on the room for this month. Please keep it for me. I am not taking my box.
Nihar

He found he did not have an envelope, so he folded the note to his father and put the other one on Vinod's mat, which he had rolled up after he had come back from the bath. Then he took the old shawl that had belonged to his mother, a pillow that had become dirtier than he thought, and a blanket he had bought, together with his razor and two towels, some soap, and a pair of white pants, a pair of shorts, a dhoti, which he had worn only at nights, and two shirts and rolled them together. He had saved a rope for just such time as this. He fastened the roll securely with the rope, leaving a doubled portion on one side for carrying. With this packing done, Nihar felt deep satisfaction. He had made up his mind to go, had written the notes, but the packing seemed to finalize the whole thing. It was done.

More than two hours passed. Nihar became nervous. He found a little shoulder bag he had brought with him; he unpacked his roll, took out his razor and a towel and put them into the bag. Then he remembered his comb, a huge pink affair, a small mirror he had left on the wall, his writing pad, and a fountain pen he had bought from a man on the street for two rupees, eight annas.

He also brought in Talat's *khadi* dhoti and loincloth, which had dried rapidly in the morning sun of Calcutta. He folded them neatly and laid them on the bag containing the Koran and the notes.

Finally Talat returned, perspiring but apparently satisfied that he had accomplished his purpose.

"Roy's taking the plane this morning. He has already left for the airport. There's no train until tonight so I have the afternoon. . . . What's this? You look as if you might be leaving."

For the first time Nihar felt strange about going. It had all seemed so right and natural up to this moment. Now with a little feeling of being caught he asked rather timidly.

"May I go along?"

Talat did not conceal his genuine satisfaction.

"Of course! I'm sure you won't regret it. I'm sorry that Vinobaji is sick, but he still talks for a little while each day. You will meet the others, and you'll see what the whole movement is about."

"You don't really know me," Nihar volunteered as a

way to make it easier for Talat to say that perhaps he ought to reconsider his decision and wait.

"What does knowing mean?" Talat asked, looking directly at Nihar. "Forget it. I'm taking you to a man who has ignited a spark in India that had almost gone out. He's ignited it in me, and it will come alive in you, too. It's terribly important. The most genuine knowing is knowing that grows in the fellowship of work for a common cause. Vinobaji said that."

Nihar was not quite sure what this meant. He did know that some of these words meant something—"ignited" and "spark that had gone out." These were words that lived, and they were knowing words, the kind of words that draw people together and make burning possible. They were words that had not lived for him all during these days in Calcutta even when he thought he had a cause. His had been a cause without a spark!

"What do you want to do this afternoon?" Nihar asked, as if the matter of his going had been settled. "You probably have a list of things you want to do now that you are in Calcutta."

"I'd like to go to one or two bookstores. I want to look at some books. I can't buy any, but maybe we can find some for free." Talat smiled, and both boys seemed happy in the agreement. Nihar had spent much time in bookstores and at bookstands in the streets, helping himself, as all young Indians do, to the pleasure of looking through books, reading portions of them, and then returning them to the stand. It is a courtesy and service bookstores seem to offer, one that all Indians accept gladly. Nihar wondered sometimes if anyone ever bought a book or magazine.

Nihar mailed his letters at the branch post office on Dharamtala Street, and the two boys strolled from shop to shop before they returned to the room, picked up their shoulder bags and Nihar's roll, and started for Howrah, a suburb of Calcutta. Nihar insisted on paying Talat's fare on the tram that took them to the station.

Nihar liked to go to the Howrah station. It was always a maddening rush of people, strange people with wonderful bags and packages. This night it was bedlam. Hundreds of refugees from East Pakistan had set up housekeeping in the vast concourse of the station—men, women, children, hundreds of children, many of them naked, most of them dirty and forlorn. Where there had always been a number of beggars, there now seemed to be a world of desperate people, not begging openly but in their eyes and faces showing the imploring look of despair. They seemed to be begging for a chance, for a home, for a break in the fate that had sent them frightened and panic-stricken out of the land where they had lived into the country where they must find refuge.

No one felt their pain more than Talat. It was from his country that they were coming, people fleeing real or imaginary persecution because they were Hindus. Nihar and Talat talked of this as they stood in the midst of this uprooted humanity, talked of Pakistan and of how Muslims wanted peaceful and good relations with India, talked of the tragedy of partition in a world that could find peace only in being one.

For the first time since he had come to India, Talat felt strange. He wanted to flee from all this. As a Muslim he had never felt any resentment toward the Hindus, nor had he known many of his friends who had. Why had all the hatred and bitterness flared up? Why were men fleeing from each other? The two boys talked about these things as they crowded into the third class compartment and found themselves surrounded by the refugees who were being moved out of Calcutta, moved to the less crowded cities, if there were any, and to the villages where they hoped to begin anew their lives which had been so tragically interrupted by the Muslim-Hindu conflict.

Both of the boys had vivid memories of atrocities. Nihar had seen people lose their senses through hunger in Bihar. He had seen the frightful ravages of people maddened by hunger. Talat had seen his fellows maddened by inexplicable fears, by hatreds that were flamed into consuming fires of killing. He had watched as his brother was stabbed and then mutilated by a mob that wreaked its vengeance on the innocent as well as on the guilty. He had seen his home and the homes of many of his friends and relatives burn to the ground.

Hunger and hatred! Both boys had seen these two destroying forces at work. As they settled down together on the floor with Nihar's roll underneath them, they found themselves pushed close together. Both suddenly became conscious of their predicament, and began to enjoy it. As they squatted in the jammed car, they came alive to the peculiar pilgrimage on which both of them were going— Talat to return to the "god who gives away land," as the village people thought of Vinoba, and Nihar to search for a savior who might call him to the devotion and dedication he wanted to give, to become the beloved disciple of a master.

CHAPTER 11

THE HOWRAH-HAZARIBAGH Express was due in Chandil just after three-thirty in the morning. For Nihar this was only the second long train trip he had taken, and he could not have slept even if there had been room. He got up when they reached Tatanagar for the fifteen-minute stop. The station platform was alive with people even at that hour in the morning. The hawkers with their hot tea, milk, gram, *pan*, and water came yelling past the *bogie* or railroad carriage in which they rode. Everyone seemed to be awake except those phenomenal men who sat or lay sleeping, seeming impervious to all the racket.

Nihar enjoyed the noise and excitement. People carrying babies, boxes, and bedrolls climbed or fell over others. Where were they all going? Occasionally he saw a man or a whole family that had been on some pilgrimage, the marks on their foreheads indicating the accomplishment of their goal. Occasionally, too, he saw a man or woman carrying a brass pot of holy water, now on its way to some village where it would sanctify and confirm a sacred rite. People were eating *chapatties*, a dirty portion of one of these pieces of flat bread was in the hands of a small child who played with it, dropped it in the dust of the car or the platform, rescued it, and then continued to eat it. There were half-naked babies whose mothers held them at the edge of the platform while they relieved themselves. There were beggars, the deformed and maimed, the blind. The beggar children slapped their little swollen bellies, going through their ritual speech of "no mamma, no papa, *baksheesh*," reciting it against the hope that someone would believe them and give a few pice, a coin almost worth less than nothing that still had monetary value to a starving person. There were holy men and well dressed men, a pageant of poverty and wealth all thrown together recklessly in the never-ending drama that night and day is seen on a railway station platform in India.

Talat had slept intermittently during the night, his head on Nihar's shoulder or in his lap. From Tatanagar on, Nihar was awake with expectancy, eager to be sure that they did not pass Chandil. When the station finally came, he had to awaken Talat, and the two of them pushed to the door and stood with their feet between a sleeping man's legs. A baby pulled on Talat's dhoti, and he stooped down to pat its head.

Talat knew the way from the station to the camp, and they walked rather briskly, their pilgrimage at an end. Nihar had plied Talat with questions. He had hoped at first that they might stretch out at the station and sleep until later in the morning. But Talat was quick to tell him that the day at the camp began at three o'clock in the morning. They found the camp alive when they reached it, and already an hour of *puja*, or worship, and meditation had passed. Ordinarily after this period in the morning, the Acharya would be on his way, had he been walking, so that by dawn he might be at some other village where he was to stop.

The boys were greatly relieved to discover that Vinobaji was better. The fever was down, and he was much stronger. The prayer meeting that morning was held so that he could be a part of it. Nihar first saw the leader lying on a mat with his head on a huge roll at one end. He had on his glasses. At first glance, Nihar thought immediately of Gandhiji. Here was the same frail body, for Vinobaji weighed only ninety pounds, the same small face and head. He seemed like Gandhi must have been. Yet here was the innovation of the Tolstoyan beard and the bushy hair that might have been handsomely curly if it had been combed or taken care of. These, at least, made him different, different, that is, from Gandhiji. What also struck Nihar was that Talat's beard was fashioned after Vinoba's.

On the walk the day before and during the first part of the train trip, Talat had told Nihar more about this new Gandhi.

"In his private as well as his public life, he is like Gandhiji," said Talat, who seemed to be full of his subject and always eager to talk about Vinobaji. "He is a vegetarian, never takes tea or coffee, and lives mostly on buttermilk and *gur*—unrefined sugar. He used to make his first speech at six-thirty in the morning and his second at the period of spinning in the afternoon. He walks, on an average, about fifteen miles a day with his followers."

Nihar had been particularly impressed with Talat's description of Vinobaji's learning.

"He knows eighteen languages, but he uses Hindi mostly. He chants the Upanishads in Marathi, and he learned Persian and Arabic when he was forty-six years old. He reads from all the scriptures of the major religions—Hinduism, Islam, Zoroastrianism, Sikhism, and Christianity. He loves the Bhagavad-Gita."

The morning that Nihar and Talat arrived, at least five

hundred people had come to the camp. The two stood listening. A young boy was singing. A man standing next to Nihar turned to him and said, "This is a Gujarati hymn. It says, 'The way of the Lord is for heroes; it is not meant for cowards. Offer first your life and your all; then take the name of the Lord.' "

After the hymn there was silence. The boys sat down. Nihar was impressed with the sense of reverence that he felt. Whether it was the sick man's presence, he did not know, but of one thing he was aware—there was a spirit moving here and it had power.

A clear, beautiful voice speaking in Hindi broke the silence. "Behold the universe in the glory of God and all that lives and moves on earth. Leaving the transient, find joy in the eternal; set not your heart on another's possessions. Working thus, a man may wish for a life of a hundred years. Only actions done in God bind not the soul of man. To the ocean of his being, the spirit of life leads to the streams of action. He moves, and he moves not. He is far, and he is near. He is within all, and he is outside all."

Nihar sat fascinated. He could understand this. He did not know the words were quoted from the Upanishads. The whining yet fascinating sitar music continued for a long period after the reading. The figure on the bed did not move for some time. At last there was some evidence of motion. Vinobaji's hand reached over to a small book. This was given to a man sitting by the bed, a man who up to this time had seemed lost in contemplation. The seated figure took the book as if he had expected to be asked to read, Vinobaji reached over and pointed to a passage. In excellent English the man read:

91

"Good master, what must I do to make sure of eternal life?"

Jesus said to him,

"Why do you call me good? No one is good but God himself. You know the commandments—'Do not murder, Do not commit adultery, Do not steal, Do not bear false witness, Do not defraud, Honor your father and mother.'"

But he said to him:

"Master, I have obeyed all these commandments ever since I was a child."

And Jesus looked at him and loved him, and he said to him,

"There is one thing that you lack. Go, sell all you have, and give the money to the poor, and then you will have riches in heaven; and come back and be a follower of mine."

But his face fell at Jesus' words, and he went away much cast down, for he had a great deal of property.

And Jesus looked around and said to his disciples,

"How hard it will be for those who have money to enter the Kingdom of God!"

But the disciples were amazed at what he said. And Jesus said to them again,

"My children, how hard it is to enter the Kingdom of God! It is easier for a camel to get through the eye of a needle than for a rich man to get into the Kingdom of God!"[1]

Nihar turned to Talat and said, "That's from the New Testament."

"Yes?" Talat replied, smiling at Nihar's pride and enthusiasm.

The first day at the camp brought a series of revelations to Nihar. There was continuous commotion with the visit

[1] *Mark* 10:17-25. Translated by E. J. Goodspeed. Copyright by the University of Chicago. Used by permission.

of the president and other dignitaries who came and went. Nihar was fascinated. This experience was completely new to him. Here, he felt again, was something alive. Something was being born that he could not understand, but it was something to which he wished to give himself. He was secretly happy that Vinobaji had consented to take medicine. When his followers had first tried to get him to take it, he had simply reminded them that the villagers were also sick and that they had no doctor. Why should he? If it was God's will that he die, he would die.

Nihar talked to several of the younger men in the camp, and he learned more about Bhoodan Yajna. He liked the emphasis that Vinobaji placed on so many things he himself thought important, especially on family unity. Vinobaji used the idea of the family as he talked with the landlords, asking them to give up land, pleading with them to think of him as an additional son and to give a share of the land to him. This was a clever idea that had worked. Even President Prasad had given some of his land in Bihar.

Nihar had watched Rajendra Prasad that day. He seemed old. Nihar had been impressed by this as he thought of what might happen to Bhoodan Yajna if Vinobaji died. Then he thought of what might happen to India if Prasad and Radhakrishnan died, both the president and vice-president seemed very old men to him. The beloved Prime Minister Nehru, too, was no longer young. What would happen to the country when these leaders died? Where were the young men, the men ready to follow those who had established the nation? Where were they? Not among the young men he had seen at Vinod's club in Calcutta. Not in the student groups he had frequented in the city.

Not even among the Congress leaders who had come to campaign in West Bengal. Perhaps they were here. Perhaps he would meet them as the days came and went in the camp. Surely from among men as dedicated as these, new leaders must arise.

Some of the men Nihar met were on fire with the mission. "We are going to establish the Bhoodan Movement all over India, in every state," the men told him. "This is the way of a bloodless revolution. Everyone can help. Even the poor have offered land from their small holdings, and some rajas and landlords have donated whole villages or their entire holdings. Nonagriculturists, too, are in this. Those who have money but no land are asked to construct wells and donate bulls, and those who have no wealth donate the gift of *shramadan*—manual labor—for tilling the land."

This social evangelist was certainly ushering in a peaceful agrarian revolution. Even before the first day had passed, Nihar had made up his mind to ask Talat if he could join, if there was a job for him. He did not care about earning money, he only wanted to be useful.

At the evening prayer meeting when Vinobaji usually talked about the message of Bhoodan Yajna, a man whom Nihar did not know spoke to the group. The villagers had made garlands, which they brought to the camp. Important men had come to offer land. The stories of the workers who had gone out asking for land and the triumphs of the day for these men were told. Then the speaker talked about Vinobaji, not as a god nor even as a hero, but as a leader. The crowd had pushed close in, as only Indian crowds can. The people were seated so thickly that the ground was a

94

patchwork of contrasting white with brown faces and legs spotting the pattern. A hush had fallen on the crowd, as if they were waiting for some announcement. Even the children who had come were unusually quiet, and only a few babies cried out in their protest against being brought to the meeting.

Nihar had seen pictures of Gandhiji's prayer meetings, and he thought this must be like those meetings, which he had never had a chance to attend. Somehow the spirit of Gandhi seemed to be here. Again and again during the day, Nihar had been conscious of it. Now as the speech was nearing its end, his attention was attracted to the man who was talking. He was telling a story of an experience at Gandhi's camp in the sweepers' section of New Delhi in 1946.

"I remember an American who came to the Ashram one day," said the speaker. "He was walking with Gandhiji after the prayer meeting. The visitor told Bapu, for that is what we affectionately called Gandhi, that he was leaving for America, that he worked among the young people of America. 'What is your message for the young people of America?' asked the American. Gandhiji smiled, remained silent for a moment and then said, 'You Americans! You always want a message. I don't think I have any message for the young people in America. If I have, it's written in my books!' But the American was not to be turned off like this. He asked again, and again he was refused. Finally just as he decided that it was probably hopeless to insist and started to turn away, Gandhiji called him back. 'I'm sorry! I don't like to turn you away like this. You want a message from me for the young people of America. I do have a message. Yes, I do have one. Tell the young people my life is my message.' "

Nihar went to sleep early that night. He and Talat were sleeping out in the open. The sky was full of stars, and a waning moon came up red-orange. There was little talk. Nihar had something to remember, something never to forget. It kept repeating itself in his mind. "My life is my message! My life is my message." Not too far away lay the little figure of a man whose life actually was his message.

Much later in the night, Nihar woke cold and stiff. He was startled because he had been sure that as he lay on his back looking at the sky the stars had suddenly started to move to the accompaniment of majestic music. With the sound they had formed themselves into a tremendous pattern spelling out across the sky the words: *My life is my message*.

CHAPTER 12

THE DAYS THAT FOLLOWED at Vinobaji's camp were filled with new experiences for Nihar. He had never read so much in all his life, around him seemed to be boys and men who were living to the accompaniment of books. He dipped into Gandhi's writings, he read in the *Koran* and in the *Gita*. He read, too, in the New Testament. He felt strange about this whole experience because it seemed so idyllic, so removed from anything he had known before. He could just go on living here the rest of his life. The companionship was stimulating, the men were of an unusually high standard. There were no little, selfish people here. If they were guilty of anything, it was an overzealousness for reform that seemed so revolutionary it could never be put into action.

Yet all the while he noticed that the talk was for a strengthening of the organization. Vinoba could not do this tremendous job alone. New workers kept coming, even some of the men whose names he had heard of, like leaders in the Socialist Party. There was even talk of the coming of Jayaprakash Narain, the Socialist leader, a man whom Nihar had heard speak in Calcutta, a man whom he remembered as having a sad face, a tired man with a strained voice and a worn-out body, reminding him of so many of the leaders he had seen. Yet this was a man upon whom millions of men depended for leadership, a man, too, whom he heard had been going through a period of regeneration and self-examination and who might give up his political leadership to join the Bhoodan movement.

The camp had an air of expectancy about it as Vinobaji grew better and became stronger. Talat had remarked that one of the noticeably different things about these people was their optimism, their sense of kismet, feeling that something was immediately ahead, something like a date with destiny that would be met. Here, for the first time since he had left his village, Nihar felt a sense of importance in living, a sense that all the gigantic problems that faced India could be solved, a sense that there was something to live for. He must talk all this out, too, with Talat.

One night while he listened to Vinoba talk about the need for one worker in each village in the country, a need for at least five hundred thousand workers who would take responsibility to become missionaries, missionaries of peace and love who would live in the villages with the people, Nihar was strangely moved. The people of India were called to a new challenge. In the new dispensation every man was entitled to five acres of irrigated or wet land or ten acres of dry land.

Still more important was the need for men to call all Indians to a change of heart. Every man was to be a trustee of the welfare of every other man. One-sixth of the annual earnings of every man must be given to the general welfare of the whole group. Cottage industries must be built up, goods coming from the mills or from foreign countries must be boycotted, and only things made in the village must be used.

Every landowner was to give up some land for the landless. Each village was to redistribute the land to those who needed it most. The villagers were to choose the people who were to get the redistributed land. Two-thirds of the new land was to be received from big landlords and one-third from the little owners. Harijans and the backward tribes were to be given first preference in the new distribution of land.

Vinoba had said firmly that collective farms like those in Communist countries were not the solution for India. The ideal he set before the campers was a realistic communism, a communism that is not based on proprietorship but on cooperative sharing. This, he insisted, is the only system possible in a democracy. He had lost his faith in parties, he said, and he had placed his faith in this movement. It would be a means of reconstructing India.

Nihar was soon filled with the idea. More and more he felt the rightness of the plan. More and more, too, he felt that he had heard all these ideas before, as if vaguely in his early life he had been associated with this plan and that now he had just been connected with it.

He found the days slipping by. His money was disappearing, even though he could live remarkably cheaply in the camp. The little village of Chandil had suddenly become a center. Never before in its history had so many people come to it, the great and the small, the seeker and the sought. The shifting populace, the day-by-day arrival of scores of people, all of this fascinated the two boys. Nihar felt himself becoming part of a movement to which he could belong. He felt its all-inclusiveness and was lost in its appeal to his devotion and dedication. Along with Talat he became one with it. The movement was positive, it had a program, and it stood for a future. There was no question here merely of criticizing the government, none of the cynicism, the ugliness, and destructiveness that had characterized Communism in Calcutta. There was no thought of subversive activity, no possibility for violence. Here was a movement founded upon love, upon respect for every man and his need and right to have a decent living.

One afternoon Nihar sat down to put all these ideas into a letter. He had made up his mind to write to Vinod and tell him that here was a future, that he should come to Chandil at once. Then he thought he might write the same letter to Nanda. She must know about the Bhoodan Yajna, and even if she did not come back from Ceylon, she could be a missionary there. He would send her literature. He started his letter to Vinod with the story of Talat, of their growing friendship in this common ideal. Then, as he wrote slowly, he became inspired by the idea that began to form in his mind. Nanda was a Buddhist, Talat a Muslim, Vinod a Hindu, and he a Christian. Why were they not a group representing different religions who could work for a common idea, for humanity?

The more he thought about this, the more excited he became. He must tell Vinoba. He wrote and meditated, and after some two hours he found that he had filled only four pages of his little pad of paper. He was amused by this, but he was not displeased. He was just about to give up his writing to go to the afternoon meeting when he saw Talat coming toward him.

"A letter?" Talat had not seen Nihar writing one before this.

"Yes, Tal, I'm writing to Vinod. I've got a great idea." Talat could see that Nihar was intense and excited. "I started to write to Vin and to Nanda to tell them about Vinoba and Bhoodan Yajna. They ought to come here. But, listen, I've just thought of another great idea."

"I don't think this camp could stand another," said Talat smiling. "But go on!"

"I was just thinking how strange it was that Vin and Nana and I should have met in Calcutta and that through a strange coincidence, Vinod should have met you and brought you home. I just remembered that Nana is a Buddhist, Vinod a Hindu, you're a Muslim, and I'm a Christian—and we can all be one in this movement."

"What do you mean, one?" Talat asked.

"Well, I mean that you can still go on believing in Mohammed and Nana can still be a Buddhist and Vin a

Hindu and I can be a Christian, and yet it won't matter, we can forget our differences. . . ."

"Because they are so insignificant?" Talat interrupted to ask.

"Exactly," Nihar went on enthusiastically, "because they don't really matter."

"Why not?" Talat came back.

"Because when you work for a common cause, caste and creed don't really matter." Nihar was pleased with his reasoning.

"That's because there is no creed in Hinduism, even if there is a caste. It's because there is no creed that there can be caste and that caste can be relegated to the outmoded and outworn. But that's not true in Islam. Look, Nihar, get this straight. I'm a Muslim, and I intend to remain a Muslim whatever you become. I don't mean to be ugly about this, but doesn't it strike you that the reason Vin and Nanda—of course, I don't know her—and you all seem so ready to find a common cause in which you can forget what you are is because you are such poor representatives of what you call yourselves, if you'll forgive me, such ignorant and ineffective examples of what you are supposed to be?"

"You mean that as a Christian, I don't seem to be a shining, outstanding example of what I believe?"

Talat had seated himself close to Nihar. He slid down in the ground at Nihar's feet. Nihar had propped himself on a large root of a tree to write.

"I mean," Talat went on, "that we've been friends for three weeks now, good friends, and I've come to be very fond of you. When I met you at the room in Calcutta, I felt something about you. I'm not sure what it was, but I

101

liked your spirit, your sensitivity. These are important in a person. I felt something that seemed to come alive in you the minute it struck what was alive in me. We felt each other. When I knew you were a Christian, I was happier still. I like Jesus as a man, and I've always felt you Christians have the possibility of being wonderful people. You needed a friend. I didn't know you, obviously, but I knew you were a Christian, that I could like you, and it would be right just because you were a Christian. Then I held out the bait of this movement before you and you bit on it like a hungry fish, swallowed it hook, line, and sinker, as they say in the West. I found you my captive. Fortunately, I'm a decent fellow, but I've wondered many times what I might have done with you had I not been so decent. You were ready for anything."

"Because I was so fed up with Vinod's crowd, with Communism, with the endless talk, always negative, always destructive. I wanted something positive, something I could believe in, something I could give myself to, something that had a constructive future, I guess you'd say." Nihar was putting into words what he had actually scarcely realized.

"Why don't you try Christianity?" Talat smiled. His knowing smile went straight to Nihar's heart. "Forgive me, Niji, you want to get straight what this Bhoodan movement is all about. It's not just an economic panacea for the ills of India. It's not a political party nor even a political ideology. It is a reform built on religion. It expects religion to give the basic impulses that will make men give up land. It doesn't work by intimidation nor by social pressure. When the landlords leave the villages when Vinoba comes,

102

he does not criticize them. He knows they are not ready to make the gift. You don't make the gift until your heart is right. This is a movement for a change of heart. It depends on religion to change the heart. It needs a religion of love."

Nihar felt everything inside of him turning over. He had not been talked to like this before. Talat went on, "I've felt for some time that Christianity was ideally the religion to give men the impetus for the movement. It needs a basis if it is to succeed. That's what frightens me about it. We, all of us, Buddhists, Muslims, Hindus, Christians, bring such a weak basis with us. We're such poor representatives of what we call ourselves. I've been studying the *Koran* as I've never studied it before, and I'm a better Muslim than I've ever been. I'm going to be a better beloved disciple. . . ."

Nihar put his hand on Talat's head. After what seemed not more than a moment, he stood up. For the first time since he had been lonely in Calcutta, tears came to his eyes. Two words had been spoken—just two words—but they were words that came like burning reminders of something in the past that had been good and beautiful. "Beloved Disciple"—the words played along the strings of memory in his confused brain and then suddenly struck a chord so mighty that its sound deafened his senses, and he felt stunned. "Beloved Disciple, Beloved Disciple, Beloved Disciple," echoed through his consciousness. The words brought back images as clear as any pictures in an album—a mela in a village, the crowds of villagers in the clear night, and before them the Master of Love and his Beloved Disciple.

He must get away. Again he felt the impetus that he had felt before. This time it was not to flee, it was to return.

103

He must go back to his village because he had met the Master and he would become the Beloved Disciple. He did not stop to say anything to Talat after he stood up. Talat would understand. He walked away. Talat stayed on the ground and did not turn around. That was understanding.

CHAPTER 13

THE TIME BETWEEN THE making and the carrying out of a resolution is not a matter of hours nor even days and years. More often than not it is a matter of keeping fresh the intensity of the desire to change. Nihar's parting with Talat on the afternoon when he had been vividly reminded of an old yearning was the moment, too, of a resolution. He would go back to his village not necessarily to act in a play but to find himself and his relationship to life in terms of work. He would study and work. Perhaps this might show him to what he belonged, of whom he was a disciple.

He wanted to be alone. His decision to return was so different this time from the experience in Calcutta. Then it seemed to be a fleeing from something, now it seemed more to be going to something. Furthermore, he believed that Christians, all people for that matter but especially Christians, ought to be concerned with Bhoodan Yajna. In many instances they were the landless ones of northern India.

Nihar sought out Vinobaji and had a talk with him. He wanted to know what a change of heart meant for him. He was surprised to hear the little man say that no one could tell another what a change of heart would mean for him, that it actually happened first inside one, that a person in whom the change took place was the only one who knew when it happened. Nihar told Vinoba that he felt sure he had had a change of heart. To this the Acharya replied that when one's heart changes, God comes in and the old selfish self moves out. You will know it, he assured Nihar, because you will know what it means to have love in your heart and you will act out of that wonderful compulsion.

As Nihar went away from this conversation, he met Talat with a letter in his hand. Before Nihar took it, he saw the stamp from Ceylon on the envelope and the address of the camp written over the Calcutta street. The letter was from Nanda. Talat smiled as he teased Nihar by offering the letter and then pulling it away.

"I'll give it to you if you will let me read it," he went on. "Promise? You know all mail is censored here. We're afraid the Communists might get onto Vinoba's system and have a change of heart!"

Nihar liked Talat's humor, but just now it seemed out of place. He grabbed the letter and thrust it in his pocket while Talat tried to get his hand into the pocket and to pull it out.

"At least tell me if she still loves you or whether she has been carried away by the romantic isle of Lanka. It's a dangerous place, I can tell you, especially if she is in Colombo. There are new ships in every day."

Talat had seen the Colombo postmark on the envelope. Nihar was too eager to read the letter to stop for more teasing. He started off. Then as if to cover his self-consciousness and his eagerness to see the letter, he turned back.

"I'll show it to you once it is censored! You never can tell with Nanda."

Nihar was indulging in wishful thinking. He wanted Nanda to write something that was personal. He hoped it might be something different from a lecture on the Revolution and caustic remarks about almost everything else. Yet when he had finally escaped to a tree where he could sit in the shade to read, he did not open the letter at once. He held it, looking at the writing, which he remembered so vividly from the little black book she had given him. He wanted to open the letter, and yet he did not want to. It might come in the way of his resolution, it might break the intention that now seemed so certain. At the same time he wanted to hear from Nanda. He had not written to her, she had not asked him to. This desire to see what she had written was stronger than the opposing idea, so he took out a small pocketknife and slit the envelope, being careful not to mutilate the strange stamps.

It was a long letter written on thin paper on which some delicately painted flowers had been stamped. Reading a letter is like listening to a piece of music for the first time. There is an initial thrill to it that may possibly never be recaptured. Still, like any piece of good music, the second or third reading is often more enjoyable, the hidden variations becoming obvious and the subtle meanings realized.

Nihar had never learned to write letters. He wrote only to his father—short, factual letters that told obvious things like times of arrival and departure, weather and the condition of his health. He had never read a letter that revealed a mood nor one that related itself to common interests. Certainly he had never received one that dealt with a mutual

106

concern, least of all a mutual understanding that might be built into affection. His own letters had always been conveyers of information.

Nihar's face showed the effect of Nanda's letter, and as he read it, he became more and more tense. He went back, read a second time, hesitated, and then went on. He began to read rapidly, skipped over whole sentences, turned from the second to the third page, looked expectantly at the end for he wanted to see the most revealing part of the letter, and then reshuffled the pages. He was perplexed. How long he sat rereading he was not sure, but even before he had mastered all of it completely, he found himself heading for the tent where he and Talat stayed. He must see Talat. Someone had to interpret.

Nothing can indicate closeness in relationship more than the sharing of a letter. Nihar had not talked much about Nanda as a person. Up to this time in this new found relationship with Talat, she had been merely a symbol, a representative of a religion and a point of view. Now suddenly she was a person who had to be interpreted, and to do this she must be shared. There was little, actually, that was not understandable in the letter.

Talat could not hide his interest. He accepted the letter without even questioning what Nihar meant when he said, "See what you make of it. I don't understand some of it."

Talat was quicker at reading, and he ran through the letter once and then again. As he finished, he threw the pages into the air, and, with an exuberance that Nihar had not seen, he exclaimed, "What a letter! Let's go to Ceylon. The girl's a poet. Here is poetry mixed with more common sense than I've heard in a long time."

107

This was both clarifying and confusing to Nihar. That was the trouble, this must be poetry and common sense. Both can be baffling, he had found. But no sooner had he admitted this than he checked himself. He had almost forgotten the person who wrote it. Imagine Nanda a poet. No, that was too much! He would show Talat what she had written in the little book. How stupid! Why had he not asked Talat to write in the book? Then Talat would have seen what Nanda had written.

Nihar remembered, too, what Nanda had said about how different it would have been to know her in Ceylon. At the time he had thought about how she, in turn, would have felt about him had she known him in his village. All of these ideas were rushing pell-mell through his mind when Talat called him back to the letter.

"Why don't we invite Nanda to come here? We need to start a movement among women, and she ought to be right. She says she's ready to come back to Calcutta at any time, having had two weeks at home."

"You forget she's a Communist," Nihar ventured to suggest, hoping that the very affirmation of this would dispute it and make it untrue.

"I don't think so. She's a poet! Poets can't be Communists, they can be Bhoodan Yajnists!" Talat was jubilant.

"Help me with the letter, Tal, I can't make some of it out." Talat picked up the sheets and began to read, interpolating where he thought the meaning might not carry over to Nihar.

Dear Nihar:
Forgive this terrible paper. It is fancy, but it's all I can find around the house. I've had two weeks at home, and

I'm ready to come back. Nice vacation this, nice place, too, for a vacation. Somehow I can't seem to think of staying here—it's just too much. My traveled friends tell me it's like staying in Nice or Monte Carlo or Hawaii. There are places like that on this earth, and Ceylon seems so much that way to me. Or maybe it's because my mother (Did I ever tell you this?) is Indian, and Indians are none too popular here. They don't seem to be citizens.

I could write a lot about the trip down and about getting home again. Why is it that you can't go home again after you've been away? Is it because your folks at home don't change and you do or at least that they don't change as fast as you do? I'm sure of one thing, you can't go home again! There comes a time you have to make home wherever you go. You carry it with you.

What a change it's been to come to Ceylon. My mother's new home in Colombo is not too far from Mount Lavinia Beach, one of the most exquisite sights in the world, I'm sure. And I've spent hours on the beach, hours when I've felt myself in another world. I can't believe that a jute mill in Calcutta is in the same world. I've escaped, for this is a place of escape, and I've turned poet. I've been writing about "this fairy isle of delight"—Lanka, and I want to share with you some of the things I've written.

Lanka seems to me like a daughter of India sitting at the feet of her mother receiving her blessing. The ocean is like a deep blue sari wrapped around the girl with the tail of the sari reaching the world's southernmost point.

The other day we went to Kalawewa, the enormous tank, a veritable lake built in A.D. 227 and stretching over eleven thousand acres. It was an engineering marvel for that time, and Anuradhapura, the ancient capital of the island, derived its water supply from this tank about fifty miles away.

We have also taken a pilgrimage to Adam's Peak, which is one of my favorite spots. If religions ever meet, they will meet here because it is a center for Buddhist, Muslim, and

Hindu pilgrims. The legends about this peak are innumerable, and it stands, in its way, as a symbol of the religious liberty that is enjoyed in Ceylon.

On our way back we visited Kandy, my old home, a beautiful city on Kandy Lake where trees are laden with mangoes and oranges, and vines in season are full of grapes. Here is the octagonal Temple of the Tooth, the center of Buddhist pilgrimage. Mama went to worship there, but I just couldn't bring myself to doing it. The noise of the clanging of the cymbals and the ringing of bells repulsed me somehow, and I went out to the gardens to think. Mama says I've changed completely. She's greatly worried about what she calls my scorn of religion. She says she won't let me go away again, and in spite of the fact that I feel so strange leaving her here without my father, I'm certain I can't stay here. I'm restless—restless for something that I don't know the meaning of.

Ceylon is prosperous. The rich are very rich, and the poor are very poor, but in the cities there is a growing middle class. The tea estates never looked more beautiful. Young independence in this island is bravado.

The Buddhists are staging a revival, run mostly by one or two priests, I'm told, but it is having quite an effect. There is the same talk here as in India: Let's go back to the ancient past, to the glorious past and revive it. Let's be *pucka* pure Ceylonese. Did I say pure? Pure, that is, if you can forget the Dutch, Portuguese, English, and Indian mixtures in our people. The boats from all the countries come into the harbor at Colombo, and each day the streets are full of Dutch or Scandinavian or English or American sailors, and the place is a riot. There is no purity any more, I'd say, unless you go back into the hills, and even there you meet the remains of Portuguese and English settlers.

They're still dancing up in Kandy, and the dances are lovely. But this island, like India, needs to have a revival of something more worth while than good old ancient Lanka

110

if we are to survive. What we need is a present quality we think existed in the past. I've come to feel that the only way out politically is a stronger United Nations rid of power blocs and all the rest. Ceylon must be a part of something bigger. By herself she is nothing.

This is already too long. Where are you? I have a strange feeling you are not in Calcutta. Write to me. Tell me about Vinod. Tell me that there is something to come back to, something to live for, something real. That's what the young Ceylonese want when they are not drunk on the surface living of this enchanted isle. You would feel it, too, if you wandered up and down the Bund, the street along the ocean. That's the main recreation of young Ceylonese, and it leads nowhere. They always have to go back the way they came. There's no destination. That's our tragedy. We can't go back to where we were, and we don't know the way forward. Our souls are homeless.

Forgive this, and if you can take it, let me know what you think.

Yours,
Nanda

Angulana, Ceylon.

As Talat finished reading the letter, Nihar thanked him and suggested that, if he had the time, they take a walk. Nihar wanted to talk, he felt he must talk, and in fairness to their friendship, he must tell Talat that he was going home.

Their conversation began with Nanda, and Nihar told Talat of their meeting at the mill, of how Nanda had come to Calcutta, of the relationship to Vinod, and of all the rest of the details of his life that he had never told consecutively to Talat. There always seemed to have been so many other important things to talk about, things that were present indicative and not past imperfect. This had been his own clever way of putting it, the idea came out of a small

111

English-Hindi grammar and reader that he had been studying to brush up on his language. Talat, whose English and
Hindi were so good, had given him the book, and Nihar
enjoyed working on it. He wanted to talk as well as Talat.

They talked of the possibility of writing to Nanda to
ask her to come to Chandil now that it seemed probable
that Vinobaji would stay here to rest for some months.
Yes, that was what they would do.

"You remember we talked of Vinod's coming here, too,"
Nihar went on. "He might come up for a holiday and get
exposed. He might catch it." Talat took Nihar's hand as
they walked, an evidence of a relationship that is so characteristic of all Indian boys. He took it now as a sign that
Nihar had come to know. Talat always did this when he
wanted to say what needed to be said but might hurt.

"You don't catch a change of heart, Nihi, you simply
don't!" It was not the kind of reply Nihar had expected.
"But I'd like to know Vinod better. You seem to be genuinely fond of him in spite of what you say about the lack
of closeness of relationship to him."

"I'd like to see if it's possible to awaken love and understanding in him. I've found it in Nanda, but I've never seen
anything more than an impersonal kindness in Vinod. You
can't love an ideology, a system, a revolution!"

Talat's loud laughter stopped Nihar. "That's an idea—
loving a revolution! I've known some girls I thought were
a revolution, but I've never tried loving them!"

"You know what I mean, Tal." Nihar was always over-
serious, and Talat's joking had been good for him. "Nanda
sort of wore the clothes of Communism, played a part, but
never really became the character. Now with Vinod it was

112

different. You never thought about the clothes he wore, he was just so much the thing itself."

"He had his heart in it," Talat proposed.

"No, you can't talk about Vinod's heart being in anything. I don't know that he has a heart. That's what I'd like to find out. Nanda never found it, though. I think she searched for it. I don't suppose Vinod has thought much about her since she left. He's too busy with the club, with arguing, with scheming and plotting how they can foul up something. I've been reading about the stopping of the trains at Howrah. My guess is that Vinod and the student group are back of that. I can't tell you exactly what it is that makes me like Vinod. I suppose it is his dedication to something. That's what I first felt in you."

"The sign that you have a heart." Talat put into words what his friend was trying to say. "It's what I've felt the Communists lack, and it will eventually be the cause of their downfall. We've got to believe in the heart of man, never forget it for a moment. It's got to be the thing we work on. Not his head, not his body even to give it food. 'Man shall not live by bread alone.' The Communists are giving him bread, at a price, and the price is not freedom as such, as you've said to me. The price is the heart of man. When you sell or barter with that, you have sold your greatest possession. It's heartlessness that's the chief characteristic of Russia at the present time. That's why the movies we see and the music we hear that come from Russia are so extraordinary. It's life without a heart."

Nihar was awakened, even startled by these ideas. Here was Talat saying what he had felt but had never been able to put into words when he talked with Nanda and Vinod.

113

"Would you say it is because the Communists don't have religion?" he asked. "Isn't religion a thing of the heart? I think Christianity is."

"Precisely!" Talat was now eager to talk. "Christianity is the greatest religion of the heart. But the wonderful part of it is that it's not just something of the feelings and emotions. I heard a Christian preacher say once that Christianity was a religion in which you felt with the mind and thought with the heart. That was what Jesus did."

"Tal, Tal! That's what I've been wanting to say! You've said it." Nihar was so excited he began to skip around. He slapped Talat on the back and then hugged him. "You've put into words what I've felt. I've never felt this way before."

"Vinobaji would call it a change of heart," Talat ventured.

"I know it is, Tal. It's what I've been living for! How does it happen?"

"It happens when you meet and love someone who has had the experience. When it comes, you find yourself."

CHAPTER 14

THAT NIGHT NIHAR DECIDED to stay in Chandil a few weeks longer. Talat made it possible for him to help in the selling of literature so that he got food, and they both went out with some of the leaders to other villages to collect land. They watched the headman of the village call the villagers together and in a disarmingly democratic manner choose the families who needed land most. Nihar saw the change of heart at work. He knew now what it meant in Bhoodan Yajna and what it could mean in himself.

He read everything he could find to read. He talked to many of the men who he felt sure would become disciples of the land-gift movement in India. He particularly enjoyed the visits, for long and shorter periods, of students from various colleges. He met Brahmin boys from good families who talked of giving up their schoolwork to join the movement. He listened intently when Jayaprakash Narain, the Socialist leader, came to tell Vinobaji that he intended to join the movement, that he thought it had the germ that might guarantee a peaceful future. The leader, Narain, told the whole camp about his change of heart.

For Nihar all this was a moving experience. He grew more and more to admire Talat for his simple devotion to what he believed, for his captivating purity, which seemed to be reflected in the whiteness of the dhoti he wore and in the clearness of his eyes, and for his intelligence, which was somehow so closely linked to his feeling that he was never merely intellectual.

Their friendship grew apace until they began to go to the daily prayer meetings together, have their times of meditation together, and then read and write together in the late afternoons and early evenings. They became inseparable, so much so that Nihar began to wonder whether his desire to stay on in the camp was a real eagerness to learn more or whether it was actually a need for Talat and a dependence that he did not wish to be without. With the coming of winter months he received a letter from his father, which brought him back to his former resolution.

Nihar had written both to Nanda and to Vinod. Nanda had written back immediately to say that she hoped to be in Calcutta by Christmas. Then there was a long period when he did not hear from her. Vinod had answered him with a post card that had been so filled with tiny writing that Nihar and Talat had great difficulty in making it out. Vinod had left the mill. He was now a Party organizer, he said, and terribly busy.

What they did read on the card was a series of innuendoes about some of the projects which, from the strange way in which they were suggested, gave the boys a notion that the Party was changing tactics. The destructive, sabotage method seemed to have incurred more disfavor than favor, and the Party was distinctly unpopular. A directive had come from headquarters ordering a change in procedure. On the address side of the card Vinod had said that they had decided to concentrate on literature, on good, cheap pamphlets that could be widely distributed. He also suggested that Nihar come out of his ivory tower, come back to Calcutta, and go to work with him. He assured him he could get him a living but little else if he cared to join.

The letter from Nihar's father had referred to his coming home. His father did not go into detail, but he did say that he thought it was time for Nihar to come home. At the end of the letter he told about the mela they were planning, a bigger fair than they had ever had before. He also said they were going to have a play on the life of Jesus. If Nihar could come, he would be of great help.

It was the first time his father had suggested this, and

116

Nihar felt that the letter was in the nature of a command. He ought to go, he told Talat the night the letter arrived. In his mind he was thinking about stopping in Calcutta to see if Nanda had come back, to pick up his box, which he had left with Vinod, and, of course, to see Vinod.

To his great surprise, Talat favored his going. At first this rather annoyed Nihar, but they had talked about it many times, and both had agreed that he should go home. The letter enabled him to settle his plans, and he decided to leave in two days. The intervening time Nihar spent in collecting more books and pamphlets and in spending as much time as possible with Talat. They found that they did not need to talk, they just needed to be together. Nihar wrote to his father that he was coming. He also wrote to Nanda at her uncle's in Calcutta, telling her his plans.

He assured Talat over and over that he would write to him. They had said the same things to each other the last two days again and again. Whenever in their genuine sadness in parting, they did not have anything else to say, one of them would assure the other he would write. They burst out laughing the second evening when both started to say this at the same time. They both hoped that they would see each other again, but they thought it might be a long time before a reunion would be possible. Secretly each of them had dreaded the farewell at the station, wishing that somehow it could be avoided. Neither of them was good at farewells!

Books, pamphlets, and newspaper clippings constituted the bulk of Nihar's baggage. As he was packing, he reread portions of the little black book, probably for the hundredth time: "Man is not on this earth only to be happy, he is not here simply to be honest. He is here to realize great things for humanity and to attain nobility." He was about to put the book into the bundle with the other things when the thought suddenly struck him to ask Talat to write in it. He knew that Tal would not reveal too much in what he wrote. He decided he would ask him to write not as if it were an autograph book but as if it were an anthology. He had started an anthology of his own by copying out passages from books, magazines, and newspapers. Tal could add to the anthology.

Nihar tried to be nonchalant about asking Tal, and Tal, good friend that he was, responded in the same offhand manner. Later in the evening when the two boys met to have their last walk together, Tal brought the little book along. Nihar was too eager to wait to read. He opened it and found Tal had written after Nanda's entry:

To realize great things for humanity one must have a God whose greatness makes humanity have the stature of greatness. Christianity can help men obtain nobility because it is based on One who was nobility incarnate and whose life is the way to love, goodness, and nobility; on One who can give men a change of heart. Now that your heart has changed, it has found the dwelling place where changed hearts work together, with each loving the other in a common task—the advancement of a kind of life on earth in which love and understanding and faith grow from God and reside in man.

I write this as one whose heart has changed to one whose heart has changed and who rejoices in the common relationship that can never change.

Tal

"Thanks, Tal," was all Nihar said when he had finished.

118

The walk that evening Nihar and Talat never forgot. It became part of both of them. The next night at the station, Nihar was glad the steam and smoke from the engine completely shrouded Talat as the train pulled out. It seemed to cause him to disappear without actually going away. And on the road as the smoke often raced by the window on which he leaned his head, Nihar felt it contained the spirit of the boy who had helped him have a change of heart. The trip back to Calcutta, uncomfortable though it was, was strangely unimportant. He was happy. He made room for a little boy to sleep, even though it cramped his leg, and he allowed an old man finally to push him onto the floor. It didn't matter. In fact, it was all right.

Nihar had been away from Calcutta a relatively short time. But he felt when he came back that everything had changed. Nothing, really, had changed except himself, yet as he walked through Howrah Station, the people seemed much more pitiful, the crowds of refugees even larger than before. Now they seemed not so much the subject of curiosity as the terrible evidence of man's inhumanity to man. Out on the street with his little bedroll heavier by the ten or fifteen books and pamphlets he had brought, he found himself walking indefinitely, vaguely in the direction that might eventually take him to the room where he and Vinod had lived. He would wait until the next day to make plans for going home. Now he had two people to see.

If a city seems to change in a short period, even though it presents the same appearance, how much more does a person change whose relationship with the returning stranger has not been kept in repair! Nihar dreaded rather than anticipated seeing Vinod. After Nihar had walked for some

119

distance, he hailed a *tonga* and asked the driver of the vehicle to take him to the old room, but not without first arriving at a bargain as to the cost of the ride.

Calcutta had never awakened more tranquilly than on this early January morning. The sleeping figures on the sidewalks were covered with motley quilts or materials that were so indiscriminate that no other use could be found for them—old shawls, burlap sacks, torn dhoties, and a variety of other kinds and conditions of cloth that defied classification. Even in this winter month a whole city was sleeping on the sidewalks.

As he rode along, Nihar remembered how he, too, had had this experience during his first days in the city. He recalled the mornings he had gone early to the little tap-tank on Dharamtala Street and bathed in the dim light of dawn on his way to the jute mill. It seemed ages ago. Cities and people are different when one is separated from them by a change in experience, even time becomes fallible and cannot be depended upon. Nihar was a bit confused about how long he had been away. Anyway, it was not a matter of time, it was a matter of something much more important in the flux of life.

As he jogged along in the cart, without knowing exactly why it came back to him, he recalled the day he had voted for the first time, the day that India had voted for the first time. It was just this time of the year, he remembered. He smiled as he thought how in his ignorance he had voted for a change, thinking at the time that change could be voted in. What he felt now was that he had been away long enough to know that change is something else, that a genuine change is something that cannot be measured by a ballot

120

nor even by relation to places, people, or time. What he knew for certain this morning as he reached Wellington Square was that he had greatly changed.

The expectation of seeing Vinod again was colored by strange misgivings. He had not heard from him for weeks. He was sure he had not moved, even though Nihar had written that he did not want to retain the space in the room with him. Ten other boys would be eager to live with Vinod, space for any living was at a premium in Calcutta. Nihar's apprehension about meeting Vinod, he knew, was not about finding him. He could find him if he wanted to. He was not even greatly concerned about the steel trunk that he had left. He remembered that it contained a few letters and strange mementos of good times, such as two balloons Nanda and he had played with one night at a carnival. He had put the inflated balloons into the trunk, space not being a matter of importance. They would have been flat long ago. He had left his Gandhi cap, which he wished he had had at Chandil, and his New Testament. A strange guilty feeling possessed him because he had not taken it. There were also one or two magazines, a bottle of hair oil he had ceased to use on his unruly hair, a broken comb, and a book on marriage which he had hidden away and about which he had never told Vinod. He counted out all of these things as he rode along slowly because he had insisted that the driver stop whipping the horse with the little cord whip, which must have stung the legs of the emaciated animal. He had changed!

He dismissed the *tonga* and raced up the steps two at a time, his roll bouncing on his shoulders. The little room was just the same except that two more mats had been rolled up at one end. His box was in the same place, but it had been buried under a collection of pamphlets and leaflets, tracts for the new order, which Nihar knew so well.

It was about six-thirty when he reached the room. The mill started work at just this time, so he felt sure that Vinod —and Nanda, too—would be at work. Then he remembered that Vinod no longer worked at the mill. At least he could not see Nanda until ten-thirty, but by the time he had a bath, put on city clothes, and rode on a bus out to Baranagora, it would be time for the morning break. He must hurry.

The few belongings of the owners of the other two mats did not betray anything about them. Nihar tried to find some evidence to reveal who they were. He even went so far as to unroll one of the mats only to find it singularly dirty but impersonal, as if any man or even a dog might have slept on it.

The man at the tea stall where he used to drink tea in the morning recognized him and plied him with questions. Nihar was amused that his main concern was how far Chandil was and how much it cost to get there. Nihar had asked the man if he intended going there, and the man said no. As Nihar walked away from the stall toward the bus stand, he was thinking that Chandil was as far as his change of heart and as costly as this change would be if it was real.

He had also heard from the stall owner that Vinod had been around that morning. On the bus he relived the many mornings and evenings he had made this trip, sometimes with Vinod, more often alone. He had planned his strategy at the mill. One of the labor relations officers was Mrs. Bose, a highly trained social worker who was a Christian.

122

He would go to her first to inquire about both Vinod and Nanda.

He had crowded onto the bus, and for the first fifteen minutes he had to stand, the low windows making it impossible for him to look out. The faces of the men with him were familiar. They also pushed just as they had always pushed and observed no rules about taking a seat except to grab one when they could regardless of who was there first. He had often felt that one of the reforms he would like to institute in Calcutta would be a consideration for others, the sense of queuing up and of observing some rules about taking one's turn in the mad scrambles in buses, at ration shops, at the post office, and even at the mill on payday.

He was happy to find Mrs. Bose in her office at the mill. She invited him to sit down and to tell her where he had been.

"I suppose you have been home," she began.

"No, not really." Nihar's words came slowly as he said this because it sounded so strange to him. "I've been to Chandil to see Vinoba."

"Chandil? Oh, yes, that's the village where Vinoba has been staying, isn't it?"

For the next five minutes Nihar gave an enthusiastic account of all that had happened, pouring out his experiences with an ardor that pleased the labor officer.

"Do you wish to start work again?" she asked.

"No, I'm actually going home now. I've come to tell you that I won't be working here again. You can take my case history from the files." Then without further explanation he asked about Vinod and finally about Nanda. He felt quite foolish when Mrs. Bose told him Vinod had left. He

123

had included Vinod's name in the inquiry to cover up his interest in Nanda. Nanda had not come back yet, at least to the mill. Her uncle was there, and Nihar could see him.

He thanked Mrs. Bose and started to get up.

"What are you going to do when you go home?" Her interest pleased Nihar.

"I'm not sure. I want to get some more education. I'm certain we Christians ought to be interested in the Bhoodan movement. I want to help all I can, and I'd like to work for a while with the movement. Village leaders are needed, and I think I could recruit them."

"The Christian youth of Serampore are having a meeting tomorrow night, and we have been talking about a work camp and other projects. Would you like to come to the meeting to tell us about the Bhoodan Yajna and Vinoba?" Mrs. Bose asked.

"Tomorrow night?" Nihar's mind worked quickly. Just so it was not tonight, tonight must be saved for reunion. Then he thought of his plan to go home the next day, and he started to say that he would have to go when he came to himself, feeling annoyed that he had even thought of missing this opportunity. "Of course I'll come, I'd like to."

"I don't suppose you have any place to stay now? My son is in Serampore College, and I'm sure he could put you up at the hostel. You know I have an apartment here on the mill compound. Why don't you come over for some coffee at ten-thirty?"

Nihar begged to be excused on the pretext that he had to go back to Calcutta. He thanked her for the offer of a room at the college and said he might accept it. Mrs. Bose sensed the concern Nihar had for Nanda and smiled.

124

"I'll get Nanda's uncle for you, or you will miss him."

Nihar waited while a peon went to the shipping department of the mill. He wandered over to the baby *crèche* and played with the children.

"Nanda is going to school," said the uncle after greeting him. "She will be home about four this afternoon."

"May I ask the name of the school?" Nihar made a quick decision that he would go to the school to see her.

The secretarial school that she attended was in the Dalhousie Square area. Nihar knew he could find it. He returned to Mrs. Bose's office, thanked her for her help, made a note of the place where the meeting was to be the next night, and promised to be there promptly at six.

"I'll stay the night if it's all right. It's rather far into Calcutta from Serampore. Will it be all right if I bring some non-Christian friends to the meeting?"

"Of course, we'd be glad to have them," Mrs. Bose said.

Nihar decided it would be hopeless to try to find Vinod at this hour. He would go to Dalhousie Square.

CHAPTER 15

WHEN NIHAR FIRST LOOKED into the secretarial school on the second floor of a building in Bal Bazar Street, he did not see Nanda. The class in typewriting was busy on a lesson, all of the students racing through a passage that they were supposed to copy in a certain number of minutes. Nanda was in the next room transcribing some shorthand notes when Nihar appeared at the door. She did not become conscious of him at first, so he had time to look at her. She was better dressed, her hair had been cut and waved, and her rather loose fitting, peasant-style, red-figured dress was most becoming.

When she did look up to see if the instructor was observing, she caught sight of Nihar. She dropped her pencil, got up, and came directly to him, holding out her hand with a straightforward cordiality that was completely disarming. It was just the way Nihar wanted her to be. The other students seemed impressed, and the boy who had sat opposite her, watching her as she wrote, showed evident consternation in his face when he saw their happiness.

"Nihar!" There was nothing else that needed expression.

"Nani!" was all that seemed necessary in reply. Their salutation was not through words, any sound would have carried the meaning of their meeting.

"I'll put my things away. Wait a moment." And with that she went to her table where she gathered up her exercise book and the pad and pen. Back with him in a second, she pulled him out of the door.

"Can you leave?" Nihar's voice betrayed his wish.

"Yes, it's time for lunch, and I don't care anyhow."

The two of them leaped down the stairs hand in hand. When they got to the street, each of them turned to face the other laughingly. Both felt natural and happy.

Nihar was aware of none of the awkward feelings he had been so conscious of in their former meetings, none of the signs of the usual kind of relationship so common between boys and girls in India that steals glances rather than gives them and carries an appearance of guilt that makes each

126

look and gesture have a feeling of wrongness. Nihar felt grown up. Something had been released in him that he could trust, and he was not afraid.

The next hour the conversation in the Coffee House rippled back and forth, scarcely any sentence was finished. It was one of those breathless hiccup dialogues in which many subjects are introduced and none is ever exhausted.

When they arose to leave, Nanda told Nihar that she had to go back for a test that might mean a job. Nihar arranged to meet her at four, then thought better of this because he wanted to catch Vinod when he first came home. So they planned to meet at five at a spot near the Victoria Memorial and walk back toward the river where they might be as much alone as anyone can be in Calcutta.

During the afternoon Nihar walked through Government Place, down Esplanade Row East, and on to Chowringhee Road all the way to Park Street. He lingered in several bookshops, stopping longest in the Oxford Bookstore. He had very little money left, so he noted down the names of books to buy later, feeling confident that one day he would own them.

He paused to watch a bird select a card out of a box for a woebegone-looking man who paid two annas to have his future picked out for him. The man could not read, so Nihar obligingly read the silly lines to him. He seemed satisfied. Nihar then rambled through the sections of lean-tos that were the shops of refugees and spent the last hour before going back to the room at the big museum on Chowringhee Road.

He reached the room before Vinod got back, so he settled down to write a post card to Talat. He had meant to write in the morning but forgot in his eagerness to get to the mill. He heard voices below and immediately recognized one of them as Vinod's. Vinod hurried into the room, obviously preparing to get some clean clothes for a bath. When he saw Nihar, he jumped on him, knocking him off the bedroll on which he sat. The two boys lay on the floor, looking at each other.

"Why didn't you tell me you were coming?" Vinod shouted at him.

By this time the boys who were with Vinod had come into the room, and both stood looking rather sheepishly at what they saw.

"Akum, Sham, this is Nihar. He used to live with me." There was no real greeting, and before Nihar could collect himself, Vinod had started to strip.

"You came just at the right time. S. A. Dange is here, and he's going to talk to us tonight. I've got to get a bath. You'll come along with us. Sure you will. My! it's great to have you back, and you'll get to hear Dange. He's speaking six times in five hours—think of it. He's a dynamo! He's terrific! You mustn't fail to hear him. We're going to three of his speeches."

Nihar was more amused than annoyed. Vinod had not changed. He was still mounted on his revolutionary steed, racing through life on the great destructive quest. Incidentally, one of his friends whom he had considered a lost cause had come back—just in time to hear a speech!

While Vinod took a bath, Nihar talked to the two boys. They were clerks in the railway offices who were living with Vinod. It was obvious that the relationship with Vinod had begun in the club and that they, too, were going to the

128

meeting. In fact, they had organized a meeting for the railway clerks, and Dange was speaking to them, too. Dange was speaking for everything and everybody.

Vinod came back with a towel wrapped around him.

"You'll stay here tonight? Of course, you will. We can talk even if it will be late before we get back. I'm going to have a chance to talk alone with Dange. Isn't that something! You'll come along?"

"Not tonight, Vin. I'm seeing Nanda. But I'll be back to sleep."

Nihar watched Vinod's reaction to this statement and felt rather relieved when he made no comment. The boys hurried through their preparations to go out. These consisted mostly of elaborate combing of hair on the part of the new roomers and the quick bath for Vinod.

"I'm sorry we have this meeting just when you've come back. Why don't you bring Nanda to the meeting? It'll be late before we get back, probably very late."

"I won't be back early either, Vin. It will be pretty late before I get back."

With this agreement, they parted. Nihar watched them as they raced off down the street. They were going to meet their leader. They were disciples. He could not help thinking of another master on another mission in Chandil and the men he had met there, especially the kind that Talat represented. As he walked back toward the Maidan, he was thinking that the quality of leaders, like the quality of all men, has something to do with the heart. He mailed the post card to Talat and then walked toward the Victoria Memorial.

Nanda was late, but after he had walked up and down

looking in the direction of the street to make sure he spotted her as soon as she came into sight, he saw her as she pushed her way off a bus and started walking rapidly toward the Memorial. He went to meet her, as if he ought not to miss any moment that they might be together.

First one and then the other talked as Nanda told Nihar about Ceylon, her family, how they had moved from Kandy to Colombo, and her trip back. Nihar had thought that he could never make anyone understand what had happened to him, and yet as he talked to Nanda, he had a strange feeling that Nanda understood. It was nothing that she said, it was the way she listened with such deep understanding.

They walked back toward the river but found no chance to be alone. In this vast open territory in the midst of a huge city, games were being played, families were out on parade, and boys and men were washing, drying off, going through all the natural functions of life. Beggars and sadhus had escaped to this place to eat food that had been given to them, pi-dogs fought over leavings of picnics.

Both Nanda and Nihar had learned to be alone in the midst of humanity, and this discipline stood them in good stead this evening. They finally found a bench that was somewhat isolated and then stood some distance from it to wait for its sleeping occupant to give it up. Nihar noticed that the man who slept there had few clothes on and that his body was thin and bony. He went over to the bench when he saw the man rise up to look around. A happy thought struck Nihar. He suggested to the man that he ought to get some *khana*, which he knew might be a *chapatti* or a little rice and a chew of *pan*. With almost too sudden enthusiasm, Nihar gave him six annas as a bribe to move. The man was so completely amazed by this un-looked-for generosity that he got up and started away. Nihar took the copy of the *Amrita Bazar Patrika* newspaper that he had saved just for this purpose and spread it on the bench. Then he bought a few annas' worth of parched grain and some peanuts, and they settled down for the evening.

That night on a park bench near Queens Way in Cal-cutta in January, 1953, a young boy and girl exchanged the thoughts of their hearts, hearts that had been changed since the boy and girl had seen each other a few months before, but hearts that because of that change now had a common beat as if they were hearing the same music. That is love. It is the same in India as in the United States or China. That the heart can be drugged by ideologies Nanda and Nihar confessed to each other. That love can be resurrected and redirected and that love can unite one heart with another, a boy and girl on a park bench in India knew for certain when a distant clock struck two that morning.

CHAPTER 16

WHEN NIHAR HAD PUT Nanda in a taxi and finally reached the room, he found the boys asleep. There was no talk, and when they rushed off in the morning, he was so deep in sleep that he did not hear them go. He did not wake up until ten, in fact. He repacked his few belongings, arranged the things in his trunk to take to the station, and in the late afternoon started for Serampore. He had spent the afternoon working on his speech, the first speech in his life. When he finally left the room, he put a note on Vinod's mat telling him that he was going home the next day and that he would write to him. That was all he wrote, it was all that seemed necessary.

He had arranged to meet Nanda to take her along with him to Serampore. One of the girls in the Commerce College lived there, and Nanda was going to ask if she could stay with her. Nanda felt sure her aunt would not mind because the family knew the girl and she had been out there before.

At the station Nihar waited by the newsstand, using his time reading in the various magazines that littered the top. He looked into some of the cheap books that gaudily pictured girls who tempted the soldiers, and he glanced through a copy of *My Magazine* that he had seen boys at the hotel reading. He listened to the conversation of two boys who discussed crossword puzzles and the fabulous amounts of money that one could get if he really wanted to take them seriously. One of the boys boasted that he actually knew a man who had won 26,000 rupees. He was sure it was legitimate. *My Magazine* and *Illustrated Weekly* were the best. As he listened, Nihar thought of the many people he had met who depended on chance, who had faith in charms and talismans, and who believed in horoscopes and fortune telling. He was impressed by the fact that he had not heard one of these things mentioned at Chandil. That proved something, he was not quite sure what!

Ten minutes before the train came, he began to be apprehensive. Nanda would certainly come. Then he began

132

to wonder if he had done the right thing to keep her out so late the night before. Had her aunt known where she was? With these thoughts running through his mind, he walked back and forth. The time had come in his life when he was not pretending any longer, he was really waiting for someone and she must come.

But she did not come. Nihar had to take the train or else arrive late for the meeting. He stayed on the platform, waiting as long as possible, and when the train started to move, he jumped on. At the Serampore station he looked again, hoping that Nanda might have gotten on the end of the train just before it started. Naturally she could not let him know and she could not walk through an Indian train with its separate compartments.

At the station Mrs. Bose was waiting for him. Her son had come with her, and the two boys were immediately in conversation. They reached the beautiful, old church facing the river where, Mrs. Bose told Nihar, some of the first Western missionaries to India had started their work. It was a strange, old place that rather appealed to Nihar. He felt a peculiar significance in coming here to make his first speech—a testimony. Mrs. Bose had asked him about the friends he expected to bring. He dodged the question by saying that he expected a girl friend who might have come with one of her fellow students at the secretarial school.

The little auditorium was full of people, and Nihar wished that something might happen to get him out of making the speech. When the meeting began, he felt as if he had been caught in something that was moving inevitably toward a given moment and that he was part of that movement and couldn't get away. He was the last speaker of

several who were to tell how young people might do constructive work in India. One was to talk about the Five-
Year Plan, another to discuss the Community Projects,
still another to describe the social service projects in the
Calcutta area, and then Nihar was to speak on the Bhoodan
Yajna movement. Between the speeches there were *bhajans*
or songs and hymns. The hymn singing immediately recalled to Nihar the wonderful times he had enjoyed in the
Christian melas at home, and he found himself joining in
several songs that he knew. It was the first time in three
years that he had sung these hymns.

He thought the first two speakers were good, but they
seemed lifeless, their speeches sounding like prepared papers
for a school club. The third speaker came alive in his
severe criticism of the young people for their unconcern.
Nihar knew that the audience was aroused when the boy
finished. He could sense it, even if he could not see it. He
suffered during the song that was sung before his speech.
He felt inadequate. How had he let himself in for this?

He heard the chairman saying that they were pleased to
have a visitor with them and that he was a disciple of
Acharya Vinoba Bhave. Suddenly an idea struck him. He
would tell about the Bhoodan Yajna movement because he
believed in it, but he would also tell about his own life, of
his coming to Calcutta and his voting Communist, of his
meeting Talat and his trip to Chandil. He would frame
Bhoodan Yajna in a life experience. He arose to speak, and
without looking at his notes he began to talk. He was suddenly free of all fear, he did not even search for words. He
spoke with complete confidence, the words came.

What did his Christianity mean? Why was it that he had

134

to go to Chandil to find a Christlike spirit—in a Hindu? Where were the young people in Calcutta or all India who were so on fire with the spirit of Jesus that they could not help being a part of the Five-Year Plan, the Community Projects, the vast resettlement of refugees, the Bhoodan Yajna movement? The followers of Christ must of necessity concern themselves with these movements. It was part of their roots. Vinobaji had said that only Jesus Christ and Buddha and Mohammed affect changes in people's lives that make them give up their little selfish desires and work for humanity. Where were the Christians doing this?

The more Nihar talked, the more convincing he became. He told about the Communist speakers, the destructive philosophy that had been drummed into him. He became dramatic in his narration.

"I left my village in Bihar with a dream—a dream to return to that village to play a part in a Passion Play. I wanted to be John, the Beloved Disciple. At that time I was a disciple of no one, and I fear I loved no one but myself. I left my village and came here. I became a disciple, a follower of Stalin and the Communism that has been established in Russia. I thought that was the way to salvation for the masses of India. Then a boy crossed my path one night, took my hand, and led me to Chandil where I found a man who is a disciple, a disciple of Gandhiji. I became excited and elated. 'I have found the truth,' I said, 'and I will give my life to this.'

"But I soon discovered that you don't give your life to anything. When you give your heart to something that is big enough to take it, you find your life taken, not given. I am going home to Bihar tomorrow to become, if I can,

135

the Beloved Disciple in the Passion Play because I've had a change of heart. I'm going up to put my heart into something great—the life and character of Jesus—and my life will be directed by it. I'll work for Bhoodan Yajna not as an end in itself but because I am sure it is necessary along the way. It is not the end. The end is the transformed heart, the redirected heart. Now I know who can have my heart. I must be His disciple!"

The audience had not heard anything like this for such a long time that it seemed stunned at first. But as soon as the meeting was over, the young people rushed up to Nihar. He was jubilant, unafraid, secure. He had found conviction in the expression of conviction, and he was satisfied.

His eyes had searched the room again and again to see if Nanda was hiding behind some taller persons in the audience. He had noticed a girl coming into the auditorium when he first began to speak. Now she was waiting to talk to him. Finally she edged up to him.

"I'm Nanda's friend who lives here. Nanda couldn't come, and she sent this note. Thanks for the speech. I'm sorry Nanda did not hear it. You were certainly convincing."

Nihar had no chance to talk with her then, and she disappeared out of one of the side doors. He put the note in his pocket and went with a group of the young people to the hostel for food. He felt exhausted, completely exhausted and yet excited at the same time. He wanted to talk, and still he did not want to.

At the hostel after eating, the young people sat round talking about Vinoba, about projects they knew, about religion, and about Nihar. When was he coming back, and would he not like to have a Passion Play for Calcutta? It might be a great Christian demonstration. He winced at this word, for he knew this was exactly what he did not want, a demonstration! What he wanted was a witness of a life through a play.

CHAPTER 17

WHEN THE CROWD HAD left, he found himself alone with David Bose. Nihar wanted to read the note from Nanda. David had shown him where he was to sleep, and he began to undress. In the excitement of his speech he had perspired, and he asked if he could take a bath. A few minutes later he was standing in the little bath enclosure, his clothes on a bench, reading the note from Nanda.

Nihar:
My aunt waited up for me this morning, and when she heard the taxi stop in front of the home, she came out expecting you to be with me. She was furious. I couldn't convince her that I was not disgraced and ruined. She ranted and raved about what was happening to girls and boys these days, saying that everything fine and good was breaking down. She insisted that I must stay home from school today, and she cried and went on so I didn't have the heart to argue. I just took it all, mindful that I had been thoughtless. I think it unwise to try to get to the meeting tonight. I've sent this note to the school this afternoon, hoping that Saraswati will get it to you. I probably won't

see you before you go. But this is not too important now. We will see each other, as you well know. I think we can still bring my aunt around. It will have to be done in the old-fashioned way. I'll get my uncle to correspond with your father. Then perhaps we can get the old folks together, and after that you can visit us. I'll meet you, and you will decide whether you want me. I'll give you a lot of silver bracelets! That's the way it's still got to be done even though the whole process is so absurd. I understand now why people in love talk about their hearts. Thanks for the heart-to-heart talk.

Someday we may just be heart to heart, no talk. That will be love. I forgot to tell you that the last thing my uncle will care about is your religion. If you wish, I'll try to become a Christian.

Nanda

As he splashed the water on his body, Nihar realized that his life had gone too rapidly these last two days. Last night and tonight things had happened. He could not call back time again if he wanted to. He felt that with Nanda as with the group this evening he had been moved by a compulsion. He could not help what he had done. What had he done? He would be glad for the train trip tomorrow. He would have time to think.

As he rode north from Calcutta the next day, his mind was confused with thoughts about Nanda, the speech, and home. He had written to his father that he would come home, and now that he was on his way, he sensed again something that Nanda had called in the little black book "destiny." He began to believe that when one acted because he felt he must, that was destiny.

As Nihar changed trains and took what was designated as a passenger train, which meant that it would stop at his village, he was happy that he did not feel himself a stranger. He carried his trunk and his bedroll to save money. He had bought his mother a sari on his way back from Serampore, and he had a shirt for his father. He had also indulged in wild extravagance and bought a box of sweets. He was returning home with exactly three rupees in his pocket. True, he had sent his father money a few times, but he had hoped that he would use it for some new tools or for better seeds.

When the train reached his station, Nihar was startled into consciousness by the name on the board at the end of the platform. Arriving at a station is so definite, so final.

He had opened the door of the compartment before the train pulled even with the small building that housed the ticket seller and the control room. He could see his father, his brothers, one elder and one younger than he. There was also a half-witted man whom his father had given refuge and who helped carry things in the carpenter shop. He would carry the luggage as the others walked to their house.

Nihar's father and the young brother seemed older, especially his father, and he noticed that he walked less briskly than he had remembered. At first Nihar thought he would stoop to touch his father's feet as a good Hindu boy would do to show his reverence and respect, but he knew that on the platform with neighbors and relatives looking on this would embarrass his father. So he embraced him genuinely and put his arm around his younger brother, and then they started walking off the platform. The older brother had jokingly said they forgot to bring a garland, the proper way to greet a new arrival. It was the kind of welcome

139

that Nihar liked, and he felt immediately that it had been right to come home.

The little house where he lived was neatly kept. A color wash had been applied lately in honor of the returning son. His mother was the same faithful person, always ready when needed but singularly able to be inconspicuous and unobtrusive when she was not needed. It was late afternoon when he arrived, and the tea was being prepared. There was a stack of *jalebis* for the celebration, and the flies had joined the feast, settling on these sticky pretzel-shaped sweets. Everything was just as he had expected it would be. They drank their tea sitting on the hard clay porch of the house, and the conversation continued until it became dark. He had not even opened his trunk, and the presents were yet to be given.

Villagers had passed, stopped, listened, and then reluctantly walked on. Children had congregated. Nihar never knew there were so many in the village. A traveler had come home, and the village was alive to the big event. Several people had brought food, and one of the old men who had worked for his father brought a live chicken as a gift.

Nihar stopped long enough to get the large box of sweets he had brought, and as people came he gave them each a piece. Some held the sweet as if it were a prize they had received, while others gobbled it down in great speed as if they feared it might get away from them. He was deeply touched when a very old woman, who had once had leprosy but had had the disease arrested in a sanatorium established by the Christians, came to bring him two small eggs that she had saved. They were all she had to offer.

The evening was a gala occasion. His sister had just had a baby, and his brother-in-law brought her for her first walk from the house immediately back of theirs. The tiny baby had weighed just under six pounds at birth, but it had a head full of black hair and a pouty little face that the family thought looked like Nihar's. They had come to show the baby and to say that on the next Sunday there was to be a christening and that Nihar was to be the god-father.

"What's his name?" Nihar asked as he held the baby.

"Nihar," said his sister proudly as if her brother were a famous person and should have children named for him. This puzzled Nihar. That night he chose to sleep outside with the men, and as he lay looking at the sky he thought about the baby. He thought, too, about the homecoming and how kind people had been. Hindus as well as Christians! What had he done to deserve it? All he could think of was that he had gone away, a dubious distinction it seemed to him. Yet to the family and the people of this little village, it was a distinction. If a man had spirit enough to leave, he became an honored citizen when he returned. This was wrong, Nihar knew. His father had stayed in the village. He had worked hard. Many men owed their livelihood to him. They had been taught the trade of carpentry and had made more money than they would have made at any other job.

His father had stuck to his job. He had watched many innovations come to the village, like the dispensary where a local boy had learned, with the missionary's help, to become a compounder. Nihar thought he would like to help in the dispensary. His father had given the ground for this little institution, which now attracted people from the villages around. Why, this was a "land gift," he thought, long before the Bhoodan Yajna movement began! He remembered, too, the time of the famine in Bihar when many people in this village had died what seemed to him the most awful death possible. He had helped his father and his brothers, as they had worked to get some food sent in by a church relief organization. He had seen his father distribute it, according to need, to Hindus and Christians alike.

Nihar could not sleep. So much more needed to be done in this village. As they were going to bed, his father had told him of the simple clay tile molds they had made and how they were covering the old thatched-roof houses with tile roofs. Then there was the talk about literacy classes. His father reminded him that 95 per cent of the village was illiterate. A primary school had been started long ago, but a high school was needed to teach adults to read and write. Very proudly his father had brought out a language chart that had been brought by a white sahib from Calcutta. It had been given to him by a man named Laubach.

Nihar had heard all this. He was sad, sad because he had failed so miserably to realize the needs in the villages. He had just come from Calcutta. He knew all along that he was coming back to the village, but he had brought no equipment of any kind, no primers to help men read, and no ideas for village programs. What had he been thinking? Why had he been so unconcerned? Here, he knew, was where the great change in India must begin. How could he have been so unaware of this great need?

If he was honest with himself, he knew that the real

answer to this lay in the admission that he had not intended to stay in the village. He had told Nanda in Calcutta that he would come back, and she was expecting him. Furthermore, how could he stay in the village unless he depended on his father for money? This he would not do. What, suddenly, had become of his old idea to save money to go to school?

Morning came before he could think through any of the problems or make any definite plans. Yet with the morning came an awakening from a sleep that had been going on for three years. Nihar had come to himself. He had come home.

He called at the headman's house that morning because his father had asked him to. He stopped to talk with men and women he met on the roads. Their stories became their needs, and their needs became the reason why he felt more and more that he must not go away.

He had forgotten, if he ever knew, what a little dispensary could do in a village like this. The young man in charge was called a compounder. He had come early on this particular morning to get his few medicines and instruments arranged and cleaned, but even before he got there, a man carrying a small boy had arrived. The boy had become too tired to walk, so the man had carried him the last five miles.

Nihar watched the compounder as he examined the rather well formed little body. He noticed that the man stopped abruptly when he examined the boy's fingers. He took a needle from his hypodermic syringe, stuck it into the boy's finger, and there was no cry of pain. He tried it a second time on another finger and there was still no remonstrance. He looked up at Nihar, then at the father and finally at the boy.

"How long have you noticed that he has not been well?" the compounder asked.

The father did not know. Then the compounder began to ply him with other questions about the family, about their health. Finally he asked, "Has anyone in the family ever had leprosy?"

The father thought awhile and then said that an uncle who had been ill used to live with them, until last monsoon season, in fact, but that now he had gone off to live by himself. The compounder probed still more until he felt certain he knew why the uncle had left, even though the father never used the word leprosy.

"You must take this boy to the leprosy hospital today," the compounder began. "You must leave him there. I will send word to the padre that you will bring him. You must tell his mother that this is necessary, and you must take the other children there at once whether they have fingers that can't be hurt or not."

The man was completely baffled by all this advice. The compounder had dealt with his type before, so he called one of the men who assisted him—a status he bestowed on the hangers-on who never seemed to be well and who had never recovered from the malnutrition of the famine days.

"Go with this man. I will give you enough money to hire a cart. See that his children are all taken to Dr. David's hospital. Understand?"

The man said that he did and excused himself to go for his shawl, this commission would take at least two days. Nihar watched the father as he sat holding the boy. He felt

144

he must talk to him because he knew the fear of the dreaded disease.

"You have probably brought the boy just in time. Don't worry. Children can be cured. But you must get the boy to the hospital at once. Be sure to take the other children, too, and they will not be sick."

The man seemed grateful both for the sympathy and the advice. He waited until the assistant came back, the letter was written, and the money given to him. By this time a girl with a snake bite was waiting. A woman with malaria and another woman with a baby also wanted attention. Nihar stayed longer than he had expected. As he came away, he was saying to himself that this was important, that it had to be done, that one could not wait until people had a change of heart.

CHAPTER 18

THE NEXT DAY, AND THE next, the needs of people crowded in on Nihar. He found his father's home a place of consultation and planning. The headman had come to tell his father that they could take part in the national community scheme and that he felt sure there would be enough money to start an evening school for adults. "We don't have a teacher," he confessed, "unless Nihar would be willing to help us."

Needs seemed to be closing in on Nihar, or were they merely directing him toward his work? Within three days the padre who lived some five miles away came to talk to his father about the mela. While the men were talking, Nihar came back from the station where he had mailed letters to Nanda and Talat. Talat had written twice since Nihar had come home. His letters were read and reread and then carefully saved. Talat had copied out portions from his reading, a bit of prose or poetry he thought Nihar would like. He had also given a running account of the days at Chandil, of the distinguished visitors who came and went, and of the plans that were taking shape to organize the Bhoodan movement in three or four provinces.

Nihar had written to Talat that he had come home and that he was overwhelmed with all that he had found. He spent long evenings writing descriptions of the needs that he had seen.

The first three days he had watched his little brother bring the mail, hoping that he would find a letter from Nanda. On the fourth day a note came to tell him that she had caught a very bad cold the night they had stayed out so late and that she had been in bed. She could not write because her aunt watched over her constantly, fearing pneumonia. This note had been written and given to Saraswati, the girl who had come to the meeting in Serampore. Nihar was genuinely pleased as he read Nanda's cryptic statement that Saraswati had been greatly moved by Nihar's eloquence. At the end of the note, Nanda advised him to send letters to the secretarial school. If she did not get back right away, Saraswati would bring them out to her.

This troubled Nihar. He wished now that he had followed his impulse to go to see Nanda's aunt. He should have stayed a day longer. Instead he had run away. Yet he knew that Nanda could handle this situation better. So he wrote this to her and suggested that when the time came he would come down to talk with her family.

Nihar had mentioned Nanda to his mother, and she had suggested that he ought to tell his father. He did not realize that the time for telling would come so soon. When the headman of the village pressed his father the next day about the night school, he felt he must talk over his future plans with his father.

The padre came that day to talk about the mela. The chief question that seemed to concern him was related to the play, which had become an established custom. The crowds had increased so rapidly these last three years that it was impossible to think of the fair without the play. The missionary sahib who had directed the drama had gone home on furlough, but a young Indian teacher had been groomed to do this job should the play be given.

The padre asked if Nihar had been in any religious plays in Calcutta. Nihar looked rather sheepish and made some remark about the whole of life in Calcutta being a play. Nothing was decided when the padre left, but Nihar had made up his mind to have a talk with his father that evening.

He was pleased when both of his brothers came to ask him to go to a wrestling match that was being held in another part of the village.

"Is Father going?" he asked.

"No," said his little brother, "he doesn't like wrestling, says it almost makes him sick."

"Then, if you don't mind, I think I'll stay home tonight. Some other time I'll go."

It would not be easy to get his father alone. He decided

he could be most successful if he suggested a walk. There was an old dried-up tank some two miles from the village, and the walk there was not too long. Nihar approached his father and found him readily agreeable. Since the other boys were going to the match, they would have their evening food early and there still would be a good three hours left before evening.

Nihar was not prepared for the conversation that began on the walk. "I have been talking to your mother about your marriage, Son, and we both think it is time you were getting married. I had a letter some months ago from my brother in Pakaur. His wife's niece seems to be a fine girl, just seventeen and a 'matric pass.' He asked me what our plans were for you. I waited some time to write back, and then I told him that when you came here, which I expected to be very soon, I would take this matter up with you. It's a good family, rather better off than most of us."

Nihar felt that he must interrupt before he heard too much, that the sooner he stopped this planning, the better it would be.

"I wanted to talk to you, too, because I've been thinking about marriage. Naturally it will all depend on what I do and where I stay. But I must tell you that I met a girl in Calcutta, a girl from Ceylon, whom I think I'd like to marry."

"A girl you met?" The old man stopped. "From Ceylon?" Both suggestions seemed incomprehensible, sensible man though he was. "An Indian girl? A Christian?"

Before there could be any more embarrassing questions, Nihar decided he must tell him the truth.

"Her mother is Indian," Nihar started. "Her father, who

died two years ago, was Ceylonese. She was brought up a Buddhist, but since she has been living in Calcutta she has given up her religion."

Nihar knew that this would be the stumbling block with his father. He knew what it had meant for his father to become a Christian, he knew that he had suffered actual persecution when he made the decision, and Nihar could never forget the pain on his father's face the day he was struck by the caste carpenter. Now a son of his was asking to marry a Buddhist—no, a son was merely telling him he wanted to marry in the tone of intention, not asking.

"I know what this means to you. But I'd like to ask just one thing of you. Don't close your mind to Nanda until you have met her."

They walked on for some time without saying anything. When they reached the tank, they sat down. Nihar began to tell about his Calcutta experiences, about the work at the mill, the meeting with Talat, the trip to Chandil.

His father stopped him when he mentioned Talat. "You wrote that he is a Muslim, and you speak as if you have a high regard for him." He went on to explain that he had had excellent relationship with several Muslims but that he had never wanted anything more than an impersonal business connection with them.

"Is Talat a good Muslim?" his father asked finally.

"A very good Muslim, one of the finest possible. I think my feeling for him is deeper than the difference you feel in religions. I don't think all religions are the same, but I do believe what our missionaries have always claimed—that first of all we are God's children, all of us, and that we can reach a place of love and understanding in spite of our

149

differences. Nanda was brought up a Buddhist. She did not choose to be one, any more than I chose to be Christian." Nihar was aware that he had shifted from Talat to Nanda.

"If you live any kind of a worth-while life, Son, you've got to make choices. Sometimes I think that's the trouble with your generation as Christians. You never had to choose, you never had to suffer to stay a Christian. You're just easy Christians—Christians by name, that's all."

"Exactly!" Nihar felt that his father was saying what he had thought in Chandil and said at Serampore.

"Our Christianity has been given to us, we've not earned it, so we don't respect it. It's true all over India, I think, from what I hear. The Communists I met are trying to earn their right to be Communists, and the members of the Bhoodan Yajna are the same way. They are giving up something. We've just not earned our right to be Christian. Christianity simply does not mean anything."

"Mine does!" His father put his hand on Nihar's knee. "Mine does! I could not let even love for a woman make me compromise with something as deep as anything about me. I've put my faith in Christ, Son. I took the chance when the chance wasn't easy, and I've not been let down. It hasn't been easy, but, if I had to do it all over again, I'd do the same thing. I'm ready now for anything—nothing could change me. I want that to be your experience. You have something neither of the other boys has. I don't need your financial help. You're free to do what you wish. I only hope it will be something that is worthy of that freedom."

"Worthy of that freedom? Just what do you mean?" Nihar thought he knew, although he was not sure he wanted to hear his father say it.

150

"I want you to do something that pays for the freedom of any responsibility for your mother and me. We've saved enough money to see both of us through, and John, too, even to an education for him. You wanted to get away to earn money for the education I couldn't then afford to give you. I didn't object because I felt so strongly you would finally do the right thing?"

"What is the right thing, Father?"

"The right thing is the thing you do because you can't do anything else. When you feel deep down in your heart, Son, that you must do something, that's the right thing."

Again there was a long silence. Nihar had never heard his father talk this way. His heart was strangely warmed, his joy was great, and he moved closer and put his arm around his father. The two men sat silently with their heads bowed, neither of them moving for several minutes.

Finally the father took the boy's hand and stroked it. "I've been praying, Nihar, not asking for anything, just putting you and your future down into my heart and not worrying because I know that God has a meaning in life for every one of us. And I'm not worried about you."

They walked home silently until they came to the little house. The village had gone to bed. As they neared home, his father stopped.

"I didn't tell you what the right thing is for you, Nihar. Put this wish about the girl down in your heart and don't worry. You will know the right thing when it must be done."

"You'll know it when it comes and you alone." Nihar had heard a little man in Chandil say these same words about a change of heart. Now he had come home, and his father was saying it about a thing called love.

151

CHAPTER 19

THE DAYS WENT BY MORE quickly than Nihar had expected. The night school was started, and the Laubach literacy charts were used. Talat had heard from a Muslim friend of his in the new Department of Journalism at Hislop College that some reading material had been prepared for new literates. Before a month had gone by, Nihar received stories to read about leprosy, sanitation, kitchen gardens, democracy, child care, and the home for the newly educated villagers.

Negotiations were started with the Community Projects and the Five-Year Plan, and the village *panchayat*, as the governing body, requested the government to make their village one of the experimental stations. New cottage industries were started, and spinning as a regular daily ritual was initiated. The mela, too, was planned and both women and men were eager to help prepare things to sell. A boys' group rehearsed a dance, and a girls' group had already become quite skillful in a drill and a song.

The play began to take shape. Nihar was asked by the director to help secure the cast.

The man who had acted the part of the Christus lived in another village, and word was sent that he was eager to do it again. One day Nihar went to visit this village without telling anyone that he was coming. On his way he stopped at a nearby village and asked what the villagers thought about the man who portrayed Christ. The reactions were all favorable. In this man's own village his padre said that the experience had transformed the life of the actor and that he had become a lay preacher, working in the fields during the week and also visiting the people and talking with them when they needed him. The report was gratifying. Nihar decided this man was the right one for the part. He had a long talk with him in a field where he found him working, and plans were made for the rehearsals. The man said that during the week before the mela he would come to Nihar's village, and Nihar promptly insisted that he must stay with him.

The woman who acted Mary, the mother of Christ, was a schoolteacher, and she, too, was willing to take part. Nihar made trips to some twenty villages in the area, talked to the headmen, the padres, the schoolteachers, and any of the men he could stop on the street.

The more he worked, the happier Nihar became. People were enthusiastic in their cooperation, more than one of them saying that they were so happy an Indian was to direct the play this year. That was an asset, an augury of the years ahead when more and more Indians would assume leadership in every way.

Nihar had written down the names of all the characters, and each day he would check off the roles the director approved. Nihar had inquired about the boy who had once portrayed John, the Beloved Disciple, and he found that it was a boy who had gone to the Agricultural Institute at Allahabad. Nihar hoped that he would be back in time to participate, but word came from the boy's father that an extension program had been started and that his son was to stay there for additional study.

The desire to play John came back to Nihar. It had been

one of the reasons for his return to the village. Should he ask to do it now that it seemed possible for him? He decided to see what his father thought the reaction of the village would be if he acted John. His father was amused at the question. He looked up, smiled, and asked, "Have you forgotten what to do about the right thing?"

Nihar wrote enthusiastic letters about the play to Nanda and Talat. Both replied jokingly that they were coming up to see it. Nihar then had an inspiration. What he wanted the mela to do was to educate as well as to inspire. He might invite Talat up to give some talks on the Bhoodan Yajna movement and, without telling anyone, he would put him in the play. He knew that the villagers would object if a Muslim were in the play. It was a risky thing to do. He must consider it further.

Then he conceived the idea of asking Nanda to be Mary Magdalene. Somehow just because Mary was the kind of woman she was, the village women did not like her, and they had refused to offer to take the part. To get the women to participate had been one of his most difficult problems. He made up his mind to ask Nanda. To his great surprise, he received a reply from her aunt saying that she and Nanda would arrive within a week and that they would stay in Pakaur where she had a relative. Nanda could come over for rehearsals since Nihar was desperate for help. She closed the letter by saying that she hoped she could meet Nihar's mother and father and that she herself might come to the play.

Nihar had not thought of this even as a possibility, and he felt slightly uncomfortable that all this had to happen just at the time of the play. To his delight, Talat also consented to come, saying that he was ready to leave Chandil and that after a stop in Calcutta he would join Nihar.

This put new zest into Nihar, and the plans for the performance were laid. They had decided to hold the play at the base of a hill just back of where the mela was to be held. They had held sunrise services on this hill, and the Christians rather claimed it as a place where they might hold a play. Nihar had used the boys and men of the villages to work on the ground that he selected for the playing area. He had appealed to men in every trade and profession for help. He had found that the missionary sahib at Pakaur had a dry cell battery loud-speaker and was willing to use it ingeniously by hiding microphones behind bushes and stones so that voices could be heard from any part of the area. The entire village—men, women, and children—were all assigned some part in the production.

One day a young man came walking up the road. Nihar had just come back from working with a group of Hindu and Christian schoolboys who had leveled off the ground for the playing area. When Nihar's mother saw the stranger, she called her son. She had been apprehensive ever since she had heard that Nanda's aunt would arrive one day and there would be the ordeal of inspection. Nihar, too, lived from day to day in anticipation of both Talat's and Nanda's arrival.

As Nihar came out from the rear of the house, he saw Talat. With a bound, he reached the place where his friend waited, and he threw his arms around him. A crowd of boys and girls quickly gathered. The greeting over, Nihar took Talat to his mother and then to the younger brother, who had come when he heard the commotion. Nihar sent two

155

of the boys down to get Talat's luggage and then ushered him into the house where his mother had prepared tea. Talat seemed to fit in somehow, and every one of the family, especially Nihar's mother, reacted favorably to him. Tea over, the boys walked out to the place of the play.

"What can I do?" Talat had entered into the spirit of the preparation.

"Do you really want to be in the play? We need another thief and someone to play Simon, the man who carried the cross."

Both suggestions caused Talat to become serious. Then he turned directly to Nihar and said, "I'd like to be a thief."

Time went rapidly. Now that Talat had arrived, Nihar was scarcely aware of the tremendous work that had to be done. The village took on a festive air. When the equipment for the Petromax lamps and the public-address system arrived from Pakaur in a jeep, all the village came to see. And as each piece was carefully put into the carpenter shop, the boys stood wide-eyed and wondering.

The day finally came for Nanda's presence at the rehearsal. Talat stayed at the stage while Nihar went to the station. When he came back, Nanda was with him, and the village was more alert to see the strange young woman than it had been even to see the governor. Or so it seemed to Nihar, who was conscious of eyes looking from every opening and of the delightful, annoying gawking of the children.

Their conversation from the station was about unimportant things, the silly things one always says when a visitor arrives. Nanda laughed when Nihar asked for the third time if she had had a good trip. The excitement of the play and of having both Talat and Nanda there made Nihar ecstatic. He was walking on air.

He had been through some strange and wonderful experiences during these weeks. The night before Nanda's arrival, a young man who taught school in the next village had come to him late in the evening. He sat for a while self-consciously and then asked, "Are all the parts filled?"

"No." Nihar had made up his mind that he would not act if he could find others to take the parts. "I'm looking for someone to play John, and the role of Simon, the man who carried the cross for Jesus, is still not filled."

"That is what I'd like to try. I've been working with the man who is your Jesus, and I've learned to love him." It was the simple declaration of a disciple. "I think I could help him carry the cross."

The man seemed so much in earnest that Nihar assured him that he could try. The new Simon came to the rehearsal the next day.

The young director needed help from everyone. He had brought plots of the action that had been left by the missionary sahib. He confessed to Nihar that he was distressed because the part of John had not been filled.

"I wish you would take it," he suggested to Nihar one evening at the close of a rehearsal. "You understand the character, you would have a feeling for it."

Nihar did not give a definite answer, yet he knew that in Calcutta he had said he was going home to be the Beloved Disciple. Now that he was home, he felt inadequate, so much less worthy of the part. He promised he would think about it.

157

Nanda made a magnificent Mary Magdalene, Nihar thought. She had to speak only a few words, so the Hindi did not matter. And Talat was completely compelling as he hung on the cross trying to look at Jesus. His long hair and beard were in keeping with the character. The Christus spoke sincerely, acted with a zest that Nihar had been wishing might be characteristic of the part. This was a youthful Christ, yet one who spoke with authority, one who was kind and understanding without being weak and sentimental.

"I could be the Beloved Disciple of this kind of man," Nihar had said to Nanda one evening.

"You must be," Nanda had answered. "It's what you came home to be."

That seemed to settle the matter for Nihar. He worked out the costume for John that he thought would be right and appeared at the next rehearsal without saying anything to anyone. And no one seemed surprised. He was the part. From the day when he had watched the first village mela to this day in 1953, he had lived through a period of discipleship. First to the unknown god of the Party for whom he had cast a vote. Next to the little figure of Vinoba Bhave and his great land gift movement. Now to a Carpenter who had been sent by God to reveal his love for mankind. Every man eventually finds his master. When Nihar appeared in the cast as John, he knew he had found his.

As the final week of rehearsals came, the play began to take shape and the atmosphere of the village was electric with anticipation of the event. No one seemed to be acting, yet an intuitive sense of the dramatic gave to each one of the characters correct emphasis. In a remarkably short time

158

they had developed an *esprit de corps* that was gratifying. Above all, the spirit of the group was such that when each rehearsal was over, the whole cast would stand silently as if awaiting a benediction. Nihar sensed this feeling, and on the night before the dress rehearsal, he broke the silence.

"We've been waiting for what I suppose we might call a benediction each night as we've finished. Day after tomorrow it will come. It will be the reaction of the audience. It will come because the people will be profoundly impressed, every one of them. You will feel it if we are successful, as I am confident you have felt it even in these rehearsals. We may be able to give new life, new incentives to Christians and to non-Christians who will come to be a part with us as the audience."

The entire village as well as the villages around felt a relationship to the performance. Everyone noticed that since the rehearsals had begun there had been no quarrels. The spirit of the play had carried over to everyone.

When Talat had first come, Nihar had discussed with him the hopes he had for the play. The padre of the neighboring village had come to see them one morning. He was a graduate of the union Theological College at Jabalpur, and he wanted to lend his support to the undertaking. He became the administrative head of the whole project. His wife trained the chorus that was to sing between the scenes. One of their friends had worked night and day on an Indian orchestra, which became one of the chief contributing factors to the success of the venture.

On the morning that the padre, Bihari Lal, came to talk to them, the three of them laid some plans that made the play an integral part of the whole scheme. In the first place

159

the padre had planned to give a series of talks in the late afternoon or early evening of the days of the mela. These, they decided, should be on the theme of the play, on the meaning for the community of the life and death and resurrection of Jesus. Then Talat had said that since he was to give four lectures in the afternoon on the Bhoodan Yajna movement, he wanted to link these with the padre's talks and the play. A visiting clergyman from Calcutta was to lead morning devotions, and the padre got off a letter to him suggesting the idea of giving the whole serious side of the mela one emphasis.

The dress rehearsal was ragged. The loud-speakers were a nuisance, and the lamps went bright and dim at the wrong moments! Yet the total pattern of the production came through. All day and all evening everyone in the village, it seemed, had worked hard. The rehearsal did not begin until after ten, and it was about three o'clock in the morning when the final strains of triumphant music had died away and the village knew that the rehearsal was over.

Nanda had been constantly helpful with the girls in the play, and she and the girl who played Mary, the mother of Jesus, had become such good friends that Nanda had finally persuaded her aunt to allow her to stay in the village with Nihar's sister. She became fond of the baby in the family and several times during the last week spent her mornings sitting with the baby while Nihar's sister went about her household duties.

Nihar had not had much time to talk with Nanda, but she and Talat had found so much in common that Talat had often joined her during the baby sitting. They had discussed Nihar as only good friends will discuss a mutual friend. At first Talat had been reticent about saying anything to Nanda concerning the future. It was Nanda who opened up the subject.

"Nihi should go to school," she said, as she swung the baby in the homemade shawl hammock that they had rigged up between two trees. "I'm so glad I came. I can see now that he fits into a situation like this, and it would be a crime if he didn't prepare himself for it."

"You think that is what he needs?" Talat had asked sincerely. "I think he ought to go to that special school at Allahabad called Literacy House. It's in connection with the Agricultural Institute extension work. I bought one of the books about literacy to read on the train, and I'm giving it to Nihi. *India Shall Be Literate* is the name of it. Nihar must go to school."

"Sushila, you know, the girl who is playing Mary, is a graduate of Isabella Thoburn College in Lucknow. She's been talking to me about going there if I can get in. When I was back in Ceylon, I met a Tamil girl who had studied there. They have a night school run by the students for the community and some village work, and they're opening some courses on writing for the new literates. I'd like to go. I'm sure I must go back to school."

"Both of you will be going back to school." Talat's tone of voice betrayed what he was thinking. "That rather settles the future for you, doesn't it?"

"Yes, Tal, that settles the future for the present, and the present is all that's important now."

These conversations had gone on in Nihar's absence, but each night Tal would relay parts of what had been said.

"Nanda's got a surprise for us," he told Nihar the night

161

before the dress rehearsal. "She won't tell me or anyone what it is."

Talat noticed that Nihar became tense. "It's not about you two, it's about someone else. She's being very mysterious about it."

When this final rehearsal had ended, all of the group stood silently waiting for Nihar and the director to dismiss them. The director said that he wanted to talk about many things, about certain mistakes that had been made, about some further coordination that would smooth out the obvious breakdowns in the performance.

At this moment Nihar asked if he could say a few words. With the director's permission, he went on to suggest that through the medium of action and words, they had been given the privilege of making these characters come to life, of making them live. He then took a little New Testament from his pocket and in the dying light of a Petromax lantern he began to read:

"In the beginning was the Word, and the Word was with God, and the Word was God. . . . In him was life and the life was the light of men and the light shines in darkness, and the darkness overcame it not." He read on until he came to the fourteenth verse.

"And the Word became flesh, and dwelt among us, full of grace and truth; we beheld his glory, the glory as of the only Son from the Father."[1]

Nihar stopped. He had wanted to pray, but he felt as if he had been praying, just as he knew all these people in their way had been praying.

"The Word was made flesh and dwelt among us," he re-

[1] *John* 1:1, 4, 5, 14. Revised Standard Version.

162

peated, "full of grace and truth." This is what acting in a religious play ought to be—full of grace and truth. The man who was to play Jesus was standing next to him, and he put his hand on the shoulder of this young man and said nothing more.

CHAPTER 20

NOTHING MORE WAS SAID, but much more was to happen. After the crews had put away the properties and the men were stationed to act as *chaukidars*, the watchmen who were to sleep at the playing area, the director had an inspiration.

"Tonight none of you need to stay here," he said to the men. "No one will steal anything from this place. Go home and get a good rest. We will need to do a lot of work tomorrow before the performance."

The men accepted the idea and left. The place was black in the night except for an orange glow that came from a very old moon that was trying to shine through the mist.

So Jesus, Mary, Mary Magdalene, one thief, John the Beloved Disciple, Simon, the man who carried the cross, and the director did not go home. Something seemed to hold them as the seven sat down on the hill on which the cross had stood. It was now about four in the morning. They talked first about their parts. Each one, even the thief, said what he could do to improve his interpretation.

What a strange company this was—these characters in

the play! What a stranger group it was as they became people in real life! They talked of this. It was Nanda who said quietly that the drama of the life of Jesus had brought them together. She went on to say that this experience might also show them the way in the future. She looked directly at Nihar, and he was strangely not embarrassed. He understood.

The first streaks of dawn could be seen when they had finished their talking. Suddenly the sky began to be pale yellow, then orange, pink, and finally brilliant red. It was magnificent.

The same thought seemed to come to all of them at the same time. It was Nanda who put it into words.

"The setting for the resurrection!" she exclaimed as she stood up.

"Of course!" Nihar was also on his feet. "Why didn't we think of it?"

The last scene in the play was played at the left corner of the big natural stage. The boys had dug out a tomb and had covered it with branches and vines. Just opposite on the right was the hill where the crosses stood. As the morning light struck the tomb, it revealed the emptiness.

"The chorus must come in facing the sunrise. It's perfect!" The director was ahead, walking through the action.

It would be a daring experiment they all agreed. Indians liked long plays. They did not mind sitting up all night watching the Hindu dramas on the lives and exploits of gods and heroes. They would not mind sitting up for this play. Furthermore, it would help the management of the mela. If the play began at nine in the evening, all the interest in the mela would be taken with the play. So they decided to begin at midnight, and by five the sunrise would be just right. Talat had proposed that the chorus could keep singing until the sky was ready, and then the glorious ending could take place. Natural lighting, he called it. The man who was to play Jesus suggested reverently that God would be taking part.

The earliest risers in the village saw a strange sight that morning as these characters, still in their costumes, Talat in nothing but a loincloth with a shawl over his shoulders, came from the playing area back into the village. When they reached Nihar's home, they saw something that startled them. In the front yard a shrouded figure slept on the stoop just outside of the door. Inside Nihar saw a light and the figure of his mother moving about. He also saw smoke coming from a *chula* in the rear of the house.

His mother had heard their voices as they came up and was just coming to the door when the group arrived. All of them, except Nanda, were naturally curious. She stayed in the background as they approached.

Nihar was first to reach the figure. He stooped over to lift the shawl from the face. The dawn made it possible for him to see the tousled black curly hair, the relaxed face. He drew back, then shouted for joy, "Vinod!"

The sleeping figure sprang up startled by the shout. As he stood up, Nihar pounced upon him while the rest of the group stood in astonishment. Nanda was the first to speak.

"Our next play is to be *The Prodigal Son*." And with that she greeted Vinod.

"How did you know about the play?" Nihar asked. "You've never written!"

Vinod turned to Nanda without saying anything.

165

"That was your secret?" Talat remembered her saying that she had a secret.

"When I got up here and saw what this all was, I felt Vinod ought to come. I told him he had to come. I wish I had thought of it sooner, he could have had a part."

"He will have now," Nihar went on, "the best part—the audience!" There were introductions all around, and Vinod suggested that it was strange to wake up and meet these characters. That, suggested Talat, was just what they hoped would happen this evening—people would wake up and meet the characters in the play!

The reason for the activity in Nihar's home was that his mother had made tea and *chapatties*. She had not slept either, and as she waited for the group to come back, she had been careful to keep the water boiling.

The morning sun was getting brighter when this extraordinary company sat on the ground consuming cups of tea, *chapatties*, and delicious mango butter that Nihar's mother had made. As the villagers passed by, they stopped suddenly at the sight of Jesus, the thief, Mary Magdalene in her red sari turned into a Palestinian costume, John and the Hindu boy with the unkempt hair and dirty dhoti. Today the Word had become flesh and dwelt among them. Today the village seemed full of grace and truth.

The two performances of the play were timed to greet the sunrise, and as the new day dawned, the hills around seemed to re-echo with the exhilarating music of a hallelujah chorus. Never had this village nor any other in Bihar seen anything like it.

In spite of the fact that most of the people in the cast got

166

little or no sleep, they did not seem to mind. Their spirits had been refreshed by something greater than sleep.

After the first night's performance when they were going back to have tea again at Nihar's, Vinod walked up the little hill of Calvary and stood there silhouetted against the sky. Nihar missed him and walked back to see where he was. He came up quickly behind Vinod and stood a little distance away. When Vinod turned he was a little embarrassed, but he recovered himself quickly and came to Nihar and put his arm around him.

"You've come home," was all Vinod said. "To stay!" Vinod knew that Nihar had made up his mind. The two boys stood facing the sunrise. What they saw was a new day. What they both knew was that one of them had had a change of heart, that it would mean a new life. After a moment as they turned to go, they saw the empty tomb. Something had been released from it that was living, that had changed Nihar. Vinod knew that. Each looked at the other, their eyes saying what they could not put into words. Then they walked hand in hand across the stage and out into the village. They had other parts to play, and their stage was as big as all India.

THE AUTHOR

Harold A. Ehrensperger went to India in 1950 for the Methodist Board of Missions to do work in religious drama at Leonard Theological College. In 1952 he worked with Professor Roland E. Wolseley in the launching of the Department of Journalism at Hislop College, Nagpur University. Mr. Ehrensperger was the first editor of the Methodist student magazine, *motive*, serving as its editor for ten years. Returning to the United States in 1953, he is now Associate Professor of Religion and the Creative Arts at Boston University and Adviser to Foreign Students and the Director of the Foreign Student Program.

THE FORMAT

The text of this book is set in Linotype Janson, a type face based on the matrices of Anton Janson, whose types were first shown in Leipsic about 1675. In recutting this fine old face, Linotype draftsmen have retained its sharpness and sparkle.

The text was set by Ruttle, Shaw & Wetherill, Inc., Philadelphia; printed by letterpress and bound in paper by Book Craftsmen Associates, Philadelphia; and bound in cloth by Charles H. Bohn and Company, New York. The jackets and paper covers were printed by Triggs Color Printing Corporation, New York.

Typographic design by Patricia Birdwood Jackson
Binding by Louise E. Jefferson

INDIA
PAKISTAN
CEYLON • BURMA

Scale In Miles

0   100   200   300   400

COPYRIGHT, 1954 BY FRIENDSHIP PRESS, INC.

Disputed Boundary Claims

DRAWN AND LITHO. BY DE MOLA CORPORATION, NEW YORK

PUBLISHED BY FRIENDSHIP PRESS, NEW YORK

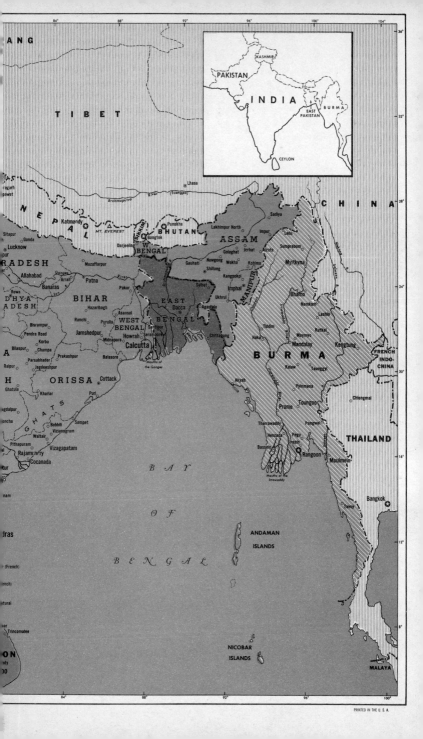